"Come to my bed tonight."

Oh, mercy. She was in trouble here.

Her body was tingling just thinking about it. All that precision. All that superhero strength. All those muscles. She wasn't a shallow woman, but the thought of getting her hands on his body made her mouth water, literally.

Bailey *really* wanted to go to his bed tonight.

But then something in the backyard caught her eye. Some kind of movement. Maybe. Bailey tried to pick through the unfamiliar surroundings and sounds. Bailey saw it then. It wasn't an animal. Nor a shadow.

It was a man....

DELORES FOSSEN

GI COWBOY

TORONTO NEW YORK LONDON
AMSTERDAM PARIS SYDNEY HAMBURG
STOCKHOLM ATHENS TOKYO MILAN MADRID
PRAGUE WARSAW BUDAPEST AUCKLAND

To Max. This one is for you.

Special thanks and acknowledgment to Delores Fossen for her contribution to the Daddy Corps series.

Recycling programs for this product may not exist in your area.

ISBN-13: 978-0-373-69536-2

GI COWBOY

This edition published by arrangement with Harlequin Books S.A.

For questions and comments about the quality of this book please contact us at Customer_eCare@Harlequin.ca.

www.eHarlequin.com

Printed in U.S.A.

ABOUT THE AUTHOR

Imagine a family tree that includes Texas cowboys, Choctaw and Cherokee Indians, a Louisiana pirate and a Scottish rebel who battled side by side with William Wallace. With ancestors like that, it's easy to understand why Texas author and former air force captain Delores Fossen feels as if she were genetically predisposed to writing romances. Along the way to fulfilling her DNA destiny, Delores married an air force top gun who just happens to be of Viking descent. With all those romantic bases covered, she doesn't have to look too far for inspiration.

Books by Delores Fossen

HARLEQUIN INTRIGUE

1026—THE CHRISTMAS CLUE*
1044—NEWBORN CONSPIRACY*
1050—THE HORSEMAN'S SON*
1075—QUESTIONING THE HEIRESS
1091—SECURITY BLANKET#
1110—BRANDED BY THE SHERIFF†
1116—EXPECTING TROUBLE†
1122—SECRET DELIVERY†
1144—SHE'S POSITIVE
1163—CHRISTMAS GUARDIAN#
1186—SHOTGUN SHERIFF
1205—THE BABY'S GUARDIAN††
1211—DADDY DEVASTATING††
1217—THE MOMMY MYSTERY††
1242—SAVIOR IN THE SADDLE**
1248—WILD STALLION**
1252—THE TEXAS LAWMAN'S LAST STAND**
1269—GI COWBOY

*Five-Alarm Babies
#Texas Paternity
†Texas Paternity: Boots and Booties
††Texas Maternity: Hostages
**Texas Maternity: Labor and Delivery

CAST OF CHARACTERS

Parker McKenna—Former army captain who joins the Daddy Corps as a bodyguard for the governor's daughter, Bailey Lockhart. Parker closed down after his wife's death five years ago, but protecting Bailey makes him see that he still has a lot to lose—and win—if he can only trust his heart again.

Bailey Lockhart—The governor's headstrong daughter and owner of Cradles and Crayons Daycare and Preschool. Even though she's in danger, she's reluctant to rely on Parker, the hot GI, but Bailey soon realizes that Parker is her best chance at staying alive.

Zach McKenna—Parker's thirteen-year-old son. He lives with his father, but they haven't really communicated in years.

Bart Bellows—The eccentric Texas billionaire and head of Corps Security and Investigation who would do anything for his old friend, the governor. But all Bart's money and influence might not be enough to save the Lockharts.

Lila Lockhart—The governor of Texas who's considering a run for the White House...but first she has to deal with the threats against her daughter, Bailey.

Timothy Penske—Lila's personal bodyguard. Bailey rejected his advances, but does he still have feelings for her, and are those feelings a part of what's happening to her now?

Sidney Burrell—The handyman at Cradles and Crayons. He's kept a secret about his past. Just how far will he go to make sure no one finds out what he really is?

Chester Herman—The mystery man who shows up in town at the same time the threats on Bailey begin. He could be Bailey's stalker...or maybe someone wants it to look that way.

Prologue

Parker McKenna stopped cold. The dinner invitation sure hadn't said anything about sharing a fancy meal with an assassin, but he was pretty sure the guy in the far right corner fit that particular bill.

"Takes one to know one," Parker mumbled to himself.

Except Parker had killed only when there'd been no other option, when it had been necessary to protect someone in the line of duty. He wasn't sure this guy could say the same.

Parker eased out of the doorway and stood next to the wall so he could take in the rest of the private dining room in the posh Dallas hotel. The Wainwright wasn't exactly his kind of place. Too rich for his middle-class army blood with its glossy marble floors and crystal chandeliers shimmering overhead.

Normally, Parker wouldn't have come within a mile of a place like this, but the invitation had, well, made him an offer he couldn't refuse. His host, Bart Bellows, had sent the handwritten dinner request along with round-trip plane tickets.

This is your chance to be part of a brotherhood again. A chance to make a difference. A chance for freedom.

Freedom.

Now, that was a complex word and not usually associated with a dinner invitation, but Parker had to admit that without that word, he might not be here. He'd probably still be in Mankato, Minnesota, supervising an apartment construction site. He hadn't felt anything close to freedom in the past five years, not since his wife's death, and until he saw that oddly worded invitation, he hadn't realized just how hungry he was for it.

Freedom from the guilt. The bad memories. From all the things he'd screwed up.

"Parker McKenna," he heard someone say. It wasn't exactly a question, and the man who approached him seemed to know exactly who Parker was.

Parker couldn't say the same. The man had black hair, a neatly trimmed beard and wore dark pants and a casual shirt. Parker was six-three, and this guy was at least four inches shorter, but there was something in his demeanor that let Parker know this man knew how to take care of himself.

He extended his hand to Parker. "I'm Wade Coltrane."

"You a cop?" Parker asked, shaking hands.

"No." The corner of Wade's mouth lifted, but the smile didn't make it to his intense black eyes. Oh, yeah. Here was a man in search of freedom as well and probably something even more. "I'm former army special ops."

So was Parker, though he was sure Wade already knew that. "Who's the guy in the corner, the one who looks ready to kill us all?"

Wade didn't even glance in that direction. He kept his attention on the center of the room where a team of tux-wearing waiters was setting up the table for seven. "That's Harlan McClain. He used to play minor-league baseball, but he was special ops, too. The non-PC term for his job title was assassin."

So, Parker had been right. "You did background checks on all the *guests?*"

Wade nodded, sipped his champagne. "Old habits."

Parker snagged a glass of champagne from a waiter who was passing by. His throat was suddenly bone dry, and he was wondering what the hell he'd gotten himself into. "I would have done the same if I'd known the guest list," Parker mumbled.

"It took some doing to get it. From what I could find out, our host invited five of us, all former military. Each of us has specific areas of expertise."

Interesting, since there were seven places being set with expensive china and real silver. Not just one fork, but four.

What the heck was he supposed to do with the other three?

And Parker obviously wasn't the only one who felt that way. The assassin guy was eyeing them as if he might use them as weapons.

"The invitation should have said this was black tie," Parker added. He was way underdressed in his khakis and dark blue shirt, but then the note as the bottom of the invitation had said *Come as you are*.

Right.

Bart Bellows was lucky that Parker hadn't taken that to heart and shown up in Wranglers and mud-caked cowboy boots.

The other guests obviously hadn't gotten the word about the hotel's dress code either because like Parker, they all wore casual clothes and they all stuck out like sore thumbs.

"I know what you mean about the black tie," Wade agreed. "I didn't expect *this*." The man made a sweeping glance around the lavish room.

Neither had Parker, though he had done a thorough background check on their host, Bart Bellows. However, in this case, background details didn't tell the whole story. Parker was sure of that.

Wade tipped his head to the wiry dark-haired man across the room who was studying them as discreetly as Parker was studying him. "That's Matteo Soarez from L.A. He worked in army covert ops. He specialized in infiltrating the enemy."

Wade slid a glance at Parker. "I think you're the only one here who actually got to protect people when you were in uniform."

Well, Parker had been a bodyguard, of sorts. A combat rescue officer. The army sent him into situations where a captive needed to be extracted or when a VIP or team leader required extra protection.

Protection.

Now, that was also another complex word. He had

three scars from bullet wounds that he'd gotten in the name of protecting others. The reminder had a bitter taste to it because Parker hadn't been there to protect the one person who'd counted most.

His pregnant wife.

And because of it, he was now on some rat-wheel guilt trip ride that he wasn't sure he could ever escape.

"The fifth guy is Nick Cavanaugh," Wade continued. He angled his gaze toward the front of the room where the blond-haired man was doing exactly what they were doing—drinking champagne and trying to figure out what was going on here. "Army reconnaissance."

Parker was betting like Wade that this Nick had gotten his hands on the guest list, as well. "So, what does a billionaire like Bart Bellows want with the likes of us?" Parker asked Wade.

"I'm not sure, but I think we're about to find out."

All the guests, including Parker, practically came to attention when the man in the motorized wheelchair rolled into the room from a side door.

Bart Bellows.

Thinning gray hair. Gray beard, too. Eyes so blue and intense that they seemed to pierce right through you.

Parker recognized the man from the numerous photos he'd found on the internet. There was no shortage of images and stories about the eccentric billionaire who was a Vietnam vet and former CIA agent.

However, most of the articles hadn't had anything to do with Bart Bellows's careers but rather his high-risk lifestyle. The man been a first-class adrenaline junkie—he'd done a stint as a race car driver for the NASCAR team he owned; he'd bungee jumped in the Grand Canyon: he'd parasailed over shark-infested waters in Australia.

In Parker's mind, Bart lived like a man looking to die.

Well, Bart had, before that wheelchair and age had sidelined him and before his son had been killed in the Middle East by an IED. But Parker didn't think it was his imagination that the old guy was still willing to take some ultimate risks.

Bart wasn't alone. There was another man who followed along behind the wheelchair. Tall, imposing. Parker figured he was another military vet or maybe ex-CIA.

"Welcome," Bart called out to them. He urged them closer with his motioning hand.

All of them, including Parker, began to stroll toward the fancy-set table. When he got closer, he saw there wasn't just silverware and china, but at each place there was a PDA.

"Take a seat," Bart invited. There was something surprising about his voice. It didn't quite go with the weathered face and his wheelchair-bound body. There was strength in that voice. Strength too in the look he gave each of them.

It was almost…fatherly.

"In case you don't know, I'm Bart Bellows, and this is Nolan Law, my right-hand man." He hitched his thumb in the direction of the person who'd come in with him.

"Take a seat," Bart repeated, and he wheeled himself to the head of the table.

Parker located his name tag. It was next to Wade's. The others did the same, and one by one they all sat down. Parker didn't know which was more intimidating—those four forks or the way they were eyeing each other. What he needed was more knives to cut the sudden tension in the room.

But Bart's laughter did that.

"Gentlemen, this isn't a funeral, so there's no need to act like it's one." Bart turned that friendly gaze on Parker. "How's your son, Captain McKenna?"

It took Parker a moment to answer. It'd been five years since anyone had addressed him by his army rank. And as for his son, Zach, it surprised him that this billionaire would even know his son's name, much less bother to ask about the thirteen-year-old. Of course, Bart was probably aware of every last detail of Parker's life.

Bart no doubt knew about Amy, her death and the unborn daughter who'd been buried with her.

Parker pushed those memories aside, or rather tried. Five years of practice hadn't helped much with that. "My son's doing good," he lied.

Bart nodded and seemed a little disappointed that Parker hadn't attempted the truth.

"We'll talk more about that later," Bart said practically in a whisper. "Maybe a change of scenery will make things better for both of you." With that cryptic remark dangling in the air, Bart looked back at the others. "First though, I should probably tell you why I invited you here. Plain and simple, I need your help."

"Help?" That came from Harlan, the assassin, and he practically growled it.

"Help," Bart cheerfully clarified. "Actually, this is a job offer. I want all of you to work for me at Corps Security and Investigations. I'll double whatever salary you're getting now and will pay for all relocation costs for you and your families."

No one said a word, but Parker could almost hear the mental mumbles. If it sounded too good to be true, it usually was.

"Yes, I did say double the pay," Bart continued. "But it's my guess that money isn't what brought you here. And it's not what will make you accept my offer. This is a chance to be part of a brotherhood again. A fresh start. An opportunity to help others and yourself."

"Freedom," Parker mumbled a little louder than he'd intended.

"That, too," Bart assured him. He made eye contact not just with Parker but with every man at the table. "Each of you has a particular set of *skills* that will come in handy in your first assignment."

"The assignment information is on your PDA," the right-hand man, Nolan, provided.

Parker hesitated but finally picked up the device, turned it on and saw a picture of the Texas governor, Lila Lockhart.

"Lila's an old friend," Bart continued. He grinned, and even though the gesture bunched up his wrinkles, his face also lit up. "And with her second term in office winding down, she's mulling over whether or not she'll make a run for the White House. Imagine that, gentleman. You could be looking at the next president of the United States."

"What does she have to do with us?" Wade asked.

"Everything," Bart answered. What was left of his smile faded. "Governor Lockhart and her family have been receiving threats. Nothing violent. Not yet anyway. But there has been some escalation. She's getting several letters a week with the same handwriting. Same tone. The person isn't happy with her current policies. Lila wasn't too concerned until recently, when someone slashed the tires on her daughter's car."

"Go to the next picture," Nolan instructed.

Parker did and saw the photo of the attractive blonde. The governor's daughter, no doubt. She had her mother's blue eyes.

"The governor's security couldn't stop the tire slashing?" Parker wanted to know.

Bart shook his head. "Her daughter, Bailey, doesn't live in Austin at the governor's mansion. She lives in a small town up in the Texas Panhandle where the Lockharts have a family ranch. Bailey owns a day care there." He paused, gathered his breath. "Lila is concerned for her children, for her hometown and for anyone who might be in the path of those who wish her harm. She asked me to provide security and lots of it."

"That's the job?" Nick challenged. "To protect an entire town and a possible presidential candidate?"

"It is. This won't be a short and sweet assignment. All of you are looking at a long-term commitment that won't end until the threats end. The job will also require all of you to relocate to Freedom, Texas."

Parker was sure he blinked.

"Yes, *Freedom,*" Bart verified though Parker didn't say a word. "Interesting name for a town, huh?"

Parker made a sound that could have meant anything, or nothing. But yes, it was interesting and so was that face in the picture. Bailey Lockhart. She looked wholesome. Beautiful.

Vulnerable.

"Mull it over," Bart insisted. And he repeated that to the others: Matteo Soarez, Wade Coltrane, Harlan McClain and Nick Cavanaugh. "If you want the job, be in Freedom in two days to start work. Until then, enjoy the hotel's amenities on the house. Since I own the place, that shouldn't be a problem."

Bart chuckled, snapped his fingers and the waiters began to pour into the room. There were at least a dozen, and all were carrying silver trays or pushing serving carts.

Parker couldn't take his attention off the picture on the PDA screen. "She's in danger?" Parker asked Bart.

Bart nodded. "Very likely." He didn't say anything else for several seconds. "I failed at protecting my own family, so Lila and her kids are like my family now. I can't fail again. Do you understand that, Captain McKenna?"

Hell. He more than understood. He was living with that kind of failure and knew how it cut right to the bone.

Parker glanced around the table and wondered if every single one of them knew that kind of pain.

Was that why they had been brought here?

Parker didn't know the answer to that, but he did know one thing. He already had enough blood on his hands. He was moving his son and himself to Freedom.

And this time, Parker hoped like hell he could stop another woman from dying.

Chapter One

Someone was following her.

Bailey Lockhart was sure of it.

She glanced around the parking lot of Cradles to Crayons Day Care and Preschool. No other vehicles were there yet, but that would soon change. In the next forty-five minutes, her staff and teachers would arrive. The kids, too. And the quiet parking lot would no longer be so quiet.

But for now, it was just her.

And her stalker, of course.

Bailey huffed. She was so tired of this nonsense. The hang-up calls. Her slashed tires. The worry all of this was causing her mother, a woman with enough on her mind since she was governor and had a state to run.

Bailey just wanted all the fuss to end. Heck, the culprit was probably just some teenager out of school for the summer and with way too much time on his or her hands. It wouldn't be a first. Her mother, Lila, had been a politician since Bailey was a kid, so Bailey had gotten used to taunts and behind-the-back gossip.

The slashed tires, however, were a first.

She took a deep breath, retrieved her purse and got out of her silver BMW, complete with four new tires. She'd outright rejected her mother's suggestion that she carry a gun. Yes, this was Texas, and the stereotype was that all Texans were armed, but Bailey didn't want a weapon in Cradles to Crayons. The children came first.

But she did grab her umbrella from the backseat. Not because it looked like rain. No. Only because she felt safer with something in her hand.

That didn't make her feel better though.

Bailey forced herself to act as she normally would. She didn't hurry toward the back entrance, her usual path to the red two-story building that was just as much home as her house was. She loved everything about the place even though she'd put it through major renovations when six years ago she'd converted it from the 1920s schoolhouse to the bright welcoming building it was now.

She nearly jumped out of her skin when she opened the white picket gate that led to the playground, and it made a creaking noise. It was a sound right out of a horror movie.

"I'm not scared of you!" she snarled, but she immediately hated the outburst as much as the stupid purple umbrella she'd brought as a pseudo weapon. This person was no doubt laughing about how uneasy she was.

Cursing her Chicken Little reaction, she rounded the corner and smacked right into someone.

A man.

He was as hard as the wall, and the impact knocked

both her purse and umbrella to the ground. Her face literally landed against the man's neck, and she was suddenly tangled up in his beefy arms.

A scream bubbled in her throat, but before Bailey could even make a sound, he shoved his hand over her mouth.

"I won't hurt you," he said.

Bailey didn't believe him. She turned, rammed her elbow into his stomach and started to run. She made it exactly one step before he latched onto her again.

"I said I won't hurt you!" he repeated.

Maybe. Maybe not. She tried to elbow him again, but he only tightened his grip and whirled her around to face him.

"Hell, no one said you'd be violent," he grumbled.

"Me, violent? I'm not the one doing the assaulting here!" But she rethought that. He wasn't making any attempt to hit her. She cursed that creaking gate and her heightened anxiety. "Sorry, violence isn't usually my first response."

"I would have never guessed that." The snarkiness in his voice made her look at his face.

She had to look up to see his face. Since she was five-nine, she didn't have to do that very often, but this guy was at least a half a foot taller than she was, and he was built like a Dallas Cowboys linebacker.

Black hair, cut short and efficient. Blue-gray eyes that were narrowed, intense. Dangerous, too, especially since he was wincing in pain—probably from her elbow jab.

Bailey suddenly wished she'd taken her mother's advice about that gun.

"Who are you?" she demanded. Too bad her voice cracked a little when she wanted nothing more than to sound like a woman who could take care of herself.

Since they were chest-to-chest, she wiggled out of his grip to put some much needed space between them, and she repeated her question. "I asked who are you?"

"Parker McKenna." And he said it as if that might mean something to her.

Actually, it did. She'd heard people mention the new guy who'd recently moved to town. This was the first she'd actually seen of him, though.

Bailey combed her gaze over him. Jeans, black T-shirt and cowboy boots. Not exactly unusual attire for Freedom, but he was somehow memorable in those unmemorable clothes. No. If she'd seen him before, she would have remembered.

She wiggled some more, creating some very uncomfortable body contact between them, but he finally let go of her. Well, sort of. When she started to bolt, he put her back against the wall and got right in her face.

"You need to listen," he insisted.

They stood there, glaring at each other. Him, still wincing a bit. Her, with her breath and heartbeat going like crazy.

Because she was so close, actually touching him, Bailey saw the moment that it registered in his eyes. She was a woman. And he became aware that her breasts were squished against his rock-hard chest.

And other things were touching, too.

He stepped way back.

"I *am* listening," she assured him, and she used some snark, too. "And what I want to hear are some answers. What are you doing here?"

"Watching you," he readily admitted.

Bailey was certain her mouth dropped open. "You're my stalker?"

That earned her a huff and eye roll. "Not even close. I work for Corps Security and Investigations."

She shook her head, wondering what that explanation had to do with her, but then everything inside her went still. "Bart Bellows owns Corps Security," Bailey mumbled. A billionaire businessman who also happened to be her mother's old friend.

Oh, no.

This better *not* be happening.

"What are you doing here?" Bailey repeated.

"Guarding you," he said in an *isn't-it-obvious* tone.

Sheesh.

Yes, it was happening.

It took Bailey a moment to get control of her temper. "My mother hired you."

"Technically, she asked Bart to hire someone, and he hired me. I was in the army for over a decade, and I have a lot of experience protecting people."

She didn't doubt that for a moment. Parker McKenna was big, strong and could probably beat anyone in a hand-to-hand combat situation.

Or chest-to-chest.

He was also drop-dead hot, but Bailey cursed herself for noticing that. He might be attractive—sizzling, even—but it was a waste of time for him to be here.

"I don't need or want a bodyguard," she stated as clearly as she could.

"Excuse me?"

How could those two little words make her sound like a fool?

"Someone slashed your tires."

"Yes. Probably a bored kid who needs parental supervision or a more appropriate hobby."

Those blue-gray eyes turned dark. "What about the hang-up calls you've been getting? A bored kid made those too from an untraceable prepaid cell phone?"

"So, he's a *smart* bored kid who doesn't want to get caught," Bailey amended. "Maybe his parents gave him the prepaid cell because that fit their budget. Lots of people use them."

At his incredulous looks, she took a deep breath and then continued. "Look, I'm thirty-one years old and run a thriving business, and I don't need my mother or her friend to make decisions about my personal security. If I feel I need a bodyguard, then I'll hire one. But right now, I just don't see the need."

She snatched up her purse from the ground, but Parker got to the umbrella first. He glanced up at the clear blue sky, gave her a flat look and slapped the umbrella into her open, waiting hand.

Bailey didn't even attempt an umbrella explanation.

She marched toward the side door. Bailey jammed the key into the lock, threw open the door and started slapping on lights. She also deposited the umbrella into the basket near the coatrack. Since she was sweating from her heated encounter with Parker, she adjusted the thermostat for the air-conditioning.

Unfortunately, she didn't think she could get the room cold enough to neutralize the effect this man had had on her.

"There's a need for a bodyguard all right." Parker McKenna was right on her heels, and he followed her inside, those cowboy boots thudding on the hardwood floors. "The black car proves that."

Bailey had already started across the reception area toward the stairs and her office, but that stopped her. She eased back around to face Parker. "What black car?"

He took a deep breath, as if this might be a long explanation, and he planted his hands on his hips. The exterior door behind him was still open, and the hot sticky breeze rushed through the room, bringing his scent right toward her.

Not sweat.

Not even the leather of his boots.

A scent that went right through her in a lust-provoking kind of way.

She cleared her throat and motioned for him to get on with whatever he had to say. For reasons she didn't want to explore, it was best to get Parker McKenna out of her life ASAP.

"The bank on the street near your house has a security camera," he finally said, "and the angle is such that it recorded the cars entering and exiting your street. I've spent hours sifting through the footage, and thanks to the Department of Motor Vehicles' database, I was able to rule out all vehicles. Except one."

"What do you mean?" Judging from his tone, this was bad news.

"Nearly all the vehicles belong to people who should be on that street. The woman in the truck who delivers your morning newspaper. Your neighbors. Your lawn guy. But there's this one car that doesn't belong to anyone here in Freedom. In fact, the plates are bogus."

He extracted something from his front jeans pocket and walked closer. When he handed it to her, she saw it was a photo of a black car.

"Recognize it?" he asked.

Bailey studied it a moment but had to shake her head. "Maybe it's a would-be burglar casing the neighbor hood." Strange, she hadn't thought that would ever be a good thing, but that explanation was better than the alternative.

He lifted his shoulder, dismissing that. "The car was in your neighborhood the night someone slashed your tires."

Oh, God. She doubted a teen playing pranks would go so far as bogus plates to conceal his identity. "Do you know the identity of the driver?"

"Can't tell from the tapes. He appears to be a white male, but he wears a baseball cap that he keeps low on his head so that it partially covers his face."

That required a deep breath. Because she had to do something, anything, Bailey straightened some wooden puzzles that were already neatly stacked on storage shelves next to the stairs.

"Ms. Lockhart, I believe you're in danger," she heard Parker say.

Maybe. But Bailey wasn't ready to accept that just yet. "Someone driving through my neighborhood doesn't constitute a danger. And the tires? It really could have been a teenager. The bottom line is I don't want a bodyguard, and that means you can leave."

"I'm not going anywhere. I moved my son here, and he's just starting to get settled."

"You have a son?" she blurted out, wishing that she hadn't. It really wasn't any of her business.

"Zach. He's thirteen." He paused and watched her fix the next row of puzzles. "His mom died five years ago, and since then I've moved him seven times. I'm looking for something more permanent for him here in Freedom."

So, the hot cowboy/bodyguard was a widower and a dad with a desire to put down roots in her hometown. Bailey hadn't pegged him for fatherhood or even marriage. Probably because he looked more fantasy material than anything else.

Forbidden fantasy, that is.

"Well, I hope Bart Bellows has another assignment for you," she told Parker. "One that can keep you here for your son's sake. Maybe in Amarillo, that's not too far away. But that assignment won't be me. Repeating myself here, but I don't think I'm in danger."

Bailey stopped fidgeting with the puzzles and headed up the stairs. She had a busy day ahead of her and didn't have time for this.

"You *are* in danger," he reiterated again. He followed

her up the stairs. "Last year the sheriff installed a camera on the traffic light on Main Street. I went through that footage as well, and in the past week the same black car has driven in this direction nearly a half dozen times."

Bailey forced herself to keep walking. "Did anyone see the driver get out and do anything criminal?" she asked, already knowing the answer.

"If they had, it would have been reported to the sheriff, and he in turn would have told you. But that doesn't mean this guy doesn't have criminal intentions."

When she made it to her office door, Bailey turned back around. She just needed to make this simple and clear. "I was sixteen when my mother first got into politics, and that means for fifteen years I've been subjected to people who don't agree with her. Sometimes those people do stupid things, and that's all there is to this. Now, please leave before the children and my staff arrive."

Figuring that was pretty good exit line that would get Parker moving, Bailey threw open her office door.

And her heart dropped to her knees.

"Oh, God," she heard herself say, though she had no idea how she managed to speak.

Parker caught her arm and shoved her away from the doorway. In the same motion, he reached down, to the holster strapped to his right boot.

And he drew his gun.

Chapter Two

With his gun aimed and ready, Parker inched inside Bailey's office. His gaze whipped to all the corners. Then to her desk that had been tipped onto its side. Papers and her laptop were now in a heap on the floor.

Two chairs had also been overturned, and the room had generally been trashed. But what was missing was the person who'd done all of this.

Parker walked farther into the room toward a storage closet.

Also vandalized.

The small adjoining bathroom hadn't escaped, either. Someone had poured out the liquid soap. And then he spotted the open window on the far wall. When he got closer, he saw the ladder propped up against the side of the building. Probably the point of entry and escape.

He glanced back at Bailey to let her know the place was clear, that her stalker was likely long gone, but the look on her face had Parker walking toward her. There was no color left in her cheeks, and her blue eyes were wide with shock. She was breathing way too hard and fast, and he didn't want to risk her hyperventilating.

Parker caught onto her and pulled her back into the hall. But she maneuvered herself out of his grip and returned to her office. She was still visibly upset, but he could see the initial shock had worn off.

Bailey stood there, her back to him, her upper body moving with her still heavy breath. She was literally the only spot of order in the room. If it hadn't been for the mess around her, she would have looked ready for a staff meeting in her perfectly fitted turquoise top and gray pants. There wasn't a strand of her dark blond shoulder-length hair out of place.

"You still think you don't need a bodyguard?" Parker asked.

Yeah, it wasn't a nice question, but he couldn't play nice here with Bailey and her safety. He needed her to understand how the slashed tires and hang-up calls could escalate.

And now she was looking at proof of that escalation.

She didn't acknowledge his question. Instead, she stooped down and reached for a framed photo.

"Don't touch anything," Parker warned. "The sheriff will probably want to process the scene for prints or other evidence."

Her hand froze, and Parker saw then that it was a picture of Bailey, her mother and her two siblings. The glass and frame had both been shattered.

Parker kept an eye on her and called Sheriff Bernard Hale. Freedom's police department wasn't exactly large or cutting edge, but he'd already had several discussions with Sheriff Hale and knew the man would do his best to find something, anything, that would help identify the person who was trying to make Bailey's life a living hell.

"The sheriff's coming out now," Parker informed her after he made the call. He slipped his phone back in his pocket, caught her arm again and took her out of the room. "Is there a way for you to get in touch with your staff and students so you can tell them not to come in today?"

Well, that put the color back in her cheeks. "That won't be necessary. It's obvious the stalker's not here. It's also obvious that his venom is aimed only at me."

"For now," Parker mumbled. "But it could get worse."

"I don't want to close Cradles to Crayons," she snapped. "I'll add security. There's a system already wired in, but we don't normally use it. We will now. And maybe I can hire you to watch the place."

Parker gave her a flat look. "I already have a job."

"That's debatable." She mirrored his flat look.

Oh, no. They weren't going back to that argument. "How can you say that after seeing this?"

Bailey opened her mouth, closed it and then huffed. "I know I sound like a lunatic, but I can't let this control my life—"

The sound shot through the room. Bailey gasped and then mumbled some profanity when she realized that it was just the phone ringing. It was on the floor but obviously still working.

"Don't go in there to answer it," Parker reminded her when she moved to do just that.

While the phone continued to ring, Parker had another look around. There were other rooms on the top floor, but nothing in them appeared to have been disturbed.

The phone finally stopped ringing, and Bailey's answering machine kicked on. "Hi, you've reached Bailey Lockhart at Cradles to Crayons Day Care and Preschool," the recorded message said. Man, her voice was downright perky. "I'm not in my office right now, but please leave a message, and I'll get back to you. Have a nice day."

After the beep, Parker heard the caller. "Where are you, Bailey?" the woman asked. She wasn't nearly as cheerful as Bailey's recorded message, but he recognized the voice—it was Lila Lockhart, Bailey's mother. "If you're there, pick up...Bailey?"

Bailey took out her cell. "I'll call her," she grumbled. "I want to talk to her anyway, about you."

But before she could do that, Lila continued, "Look, I know you're probably angry about the bodyguard I hired, but it was necessary. And I knew you'd be too stubborn to hire him yourself. How did I possibly give birth to such a bullheaded daughter who won't listen to reason?"

Bailey's mouth tightened. Her eyes narrowed a bit.

"Oh, well," Lila added. "You're obviously in a snit right now, but get over it, sweetheart. It's not as if I saddled you with a Neanderthal. Bart sent me Parker McKenna's photo and his bio. In addition to being incredibly easy on the eyes, he's a decorated army officer...."

Hell. Parker didn't need to hear this, and judging from Bailey's expression, her mother's opinion of his looks and his military record weren't helping with his argument to convince her that she did indeed need him.

"I'll wait downstairs for Sheriff Hale," Parker mumbled to Bailey.

But on the way down the steps, he could still hear Lila's voice oozing through the answering machine. "Parker took a bullet for the Under Secretary of Defense a few years ago when things went bad on a hush-hush visit to the Middle East. It shouldn't be too difficult having him around. In fact, he's a good catch, and you're not getting any younger—"

Thankfully, the machine clipped off the rest of what the governor had to say. Also thankfully, Parker heard someone at the front door. Probably the sheriff who could take a stab at talking some sense into Bailey. But when he looked out the small sidelight window, he didn't see Sheriff Hale. He saw the woman with red hair fumbling with her keys.

Parker unlocked the door and opened it. The woman went stiff when she saw his gun, and she sucked in her breath. "Who are you?"

"Parker McKenna. I'm Bailey's bodyguard. Who are you?"

"Charlotte Manning. I work here, and I usually come in through the back entrance, but I wanted to see Bailey first. Where is she? Is she all right?"

Since this woman didn't seem much a threat, Parker put his gun back in his boot holster and hitched his thumb toward the stairs. "She's in her office. Someone broke in and vandalized it."

"A break-in?" However, Charlotte didn't wait for him

to confirm it or that Bailey was all right. She mumbled an *Oh, God* and went racing up the stairs.

Hopefully, this Charlotte Manning could make Bailey understand how serious this situation was.

And another possible ally arrived.

Parker saw the sheriff's car pull to a quick stop in front of the building. Parker recognized the African-American man who exited. Sheriff Bernard Hale. He was in his late forties and had been sheriff for years. Plenty of experience and he knew Bailey. Hopefully, he could accomplish more than her mother's call had.

"Captain McKenna," Bernard greeted when the sheriff reached the front door, and he shook Parker's hand. "Good to see you again."

"Parker," he offered.

"I got over here as fast as I could. You think this is related to that car you showed me on the surveillance film?" the sheriff asked.

"Yeah, I think it probably is." And he was about to give the sheriff what few details he knew about the break-in. However, his phone rang, and when Parker saw the identity of the caller, he knew he had to answer it. "Bailey's upstairs. If you need me, just let me know."

"Zach?" Parker answered the moment the sheriff stepped away. "What's wrong?"

The question was a given, especially since his son rarely called him. Heck, Zach rarely spoke to him, especially since this move to Freedom. Parker loved his son more than life itself, but he was positive Zach didn't feel the same about him.

"You forgot to leave the money for basketball camp,"

Zach snarled. Or maybe it wasn't a snarl. Come to think of it, that was the only tone Parker had heard his son use in years.

Parker groaned. Yes, he had forgotten, though Zach had left him a reminder note taped to the fridge. His son needed twenty-five dollars for a half-day camp being held at the town's community center.

"You said I could go," Zach accused. "You said you'd leave the money."

Yes, he had—Zach's request and his approval had also been delivered in notes they'd left for each other. And Parker had meant to put the money on the kitchen counter, but this morning he'd gotten caught up viewing those surveillance disks, and then he had rushed out of the house so he could follow Bailey from her home to work. He'd been doing that for over a week now in the hopes of not just protecting her but also catching her stalker.

"I'm at Cradles to Crayons on Main Street," Parker explained. He heard footsteps behind him, turned and spotted Bailey and Charlotte making their way down the stairs. "And I can't leave right now. I'm on the job." Whether Bailey considered it a job or not.

Parker obviously couldn't see his son's face, but he heard Zach's silent disapproval. Of course, Zach disapproved of everything, so this was nothing new. "I'll ride my bike over there and get it."

Since their new house was only a quarter mile away, Parker couldn't object. Well, he could because he was always worried when Zach was on his bike and near traffic.

Heck, he was always worried about him, period.

But he wanted Zach to attend that camp. It was a chance for him to meet some new friends before school started in mid-August, just six weeks away. God knew his son needed someone to help him adjust to the move and yet another new school.

"Zach, when you get here, don't come inside." Parker didn't want Zach underfoot during the sheriff's investigation, not that his son would want to be underfoot anyway. "I'll meet you on the porch. Oh, and remember to wear your helmet and watch out for cars."

"Right." More of the snarling tone, and he hung up.

"Your son's coming here?" he heard Bailey ask.

"He won't stay long," Parker settled for saying. He hadn't wanted her to hear any of that conversation. "Have you changed your mind about closing down for the day?"

"No." Bailey folded her arms over her chest and shook her head, causing her silver hoop earrings to dangle against her hair and ears. "It's too late to call everyone. Parents are already on their way. Besides, if the children don't come here, a lot of the parents would have to miss work." She glanced at Charlotte as if seeking approval.

Charlotte didn't exactly give that approval. She looked shaken up, and rightfully so. "I need to go to the preschool and unlock the door."

Parker knew the preschool section was in the back of the building, an addition that Bailey had added on to accommodate the classes. "You can't access the preschool from inside this building?"

Charlotte shook her head. "We have a door that leads from here to there, but it's blocked off right now for a construction project. We're adding another bathroom. It's no big deal. I'll just go outside and around back."

"I'll go with you so I can make sure no one broke into that area," Parker offered.

"If they had broken in, it would have set off the security alarms," Charlotte explained. "And the company that monitors it would have called either Bailey or me."

"You use the security system?" Parker asked.

Charlotte nodded. "Just in that area and the basement. It has its own separate system that was added when it was built. We have a lot of computers and other equipment, and what with the older kids out of school for summer break, I didn't want to tempt anyone with sticky fingers."

"Smart move." Parker made sure he looked at Bailey when he said that.

Charlotte gave Bailey's arm a pat and shot him a glare, probably for the insult he'd just given her boss, and Charlotte headed back out the front door. Parker didn't close it behind her because he wanted to watch for Zach. It wouldn't take his son long to get here.

"Did the sheriff find anything yet?" Parker asked Bailey.

"No." She looked up at him, shrugged. "But we might get lucky."

"You already were lucky. Lucky that you weren't here when your stalker broke in."

Though Parker doubted that would have happened. No. This guy was a coward and had waited until a time when he was sure he wouldn't be caught. However, that didn't mean he couldn't be very dangerous.

Bailey blinked hard, and he realized she was blinking back tears. "I can't let this control me. I can't let my mother do that, either. You don't know her. She's a good woman, and she's been good for the state of Texas, but when it comes to her kids, especially me, she's a micromanaging control freak."

"That bad, huh?" Parker mumbled. "Well, at least she didn't hire a Neanderthal to protect you."

It wasn't the right time to attempt anything light. He didn't need to be defusing this situation even in the smallest kind of way. He wanted Bailey to be afraid so she would turn to him for protection. That was the plan, anyway. But after watching her fight those tears, his plan had gone south.

Parker cursed what he was about to do but did it anyway. He slipped his arm around Bailey and pulled her closer to him. She put up a token resistance and shoved her fist against his chest, but she didn't step away.

"I know you must be good at your job," Bailey said, her voice barely louder than a whisper. She spoke with her mouth right against his shoulder. "But if I allow you to stay, it's as if I'm letting my mother win this battle of wills."

He leaned his head down so that the corner of his eye met the corner of hers. "So, let me get this straight. You'd rather win than be safe?"

Bailey stared up at him. She also huffed. "You have

a knack for making me feel like an idiot, you know that?"

"Really? Because I didn't think I was getting anywhere with you."

"You're not getting anywhere," she snapped. "Other than the making-me-feel-like-an-idiot part. I've already said I'll take precautions—"

When she stopped, Parker followed her gaze.

His son, with helmet in hand and his bike propped against the steps, was standing there on the porch. And he was eyeing the close contact between Bailey and Parker.

"Zach," Parker managed to say. "You're here already."

"Zach?" Bailey repeated. She jerked away from Parker. "Uh, this is nothing. I'm just a little upset, and your dad lent me his shoulder."

"Okay." Zach couldn't have possibly sounded more disinterested, but he still volleyed strange looks between the two.

Probably because he'd never seen his dad close to a woman.

Parker had dated a little in the last year or two, but he had never brought women home and never introduced them to Zach. He didn't want his son thinking he'd gotten over his mother's death. That might feel like a betrayal to her memory.

"The money," Parker remembered, fishing through his back jeans pocket for his wallet.

"You're Bailey Lockhart," Zach said, dodging eye contact with both Parker and her. "I saw a picture of you in the gym at the community center. You were, like, young then. I mean, not like you are now."

Parker didn't know who winced more—him or his son.

Bailey smiled, though Parker was sure it was forced. "I played basketball in high school and college. Freedom doesn't have many so-called star athletes, so I made the cut and got my picture on the wall."

Parker knew she'd been an athlete. It was his job to study her background, but he was surprised that his son even had a clue who she was.

"What position did you play?" Zach asked, idly taking the money from Parker. He was making eye contact—with Bailey.

"Point guard. How about you?"

"Off guard, but if I grow a few more inches, I can move to forward. I've already checked out the other guys who'll be on the team, and there's only one who's taller than me."

"Josh Bracken," Bailey provided, and that prompted Zach to nod. "His dad is a deputy sheriff."

The corner of Zach's mouth lifted just a fraction. "Yeah. Josh is good, too. There was a basketball hoop already in the driveway when we moved in so Josh has been coming over so we can practice. He's got a wicked outside shot."

Parker just stared at them. This was the most he'd heard Zach speak in a year. Of course, he wasn't actually speaking with him but rather Bailey.

Bailey smiled again, and this time it didn't seem forced at all. "Well, since you're the spitting image of your dad, I'm betting you'll inherit his height, too. It won't be long before you're eye to eye with him and can play forward."

Zach glanced at Parker. No more partial smile. In fact, no smile at all. His normal scowl returned. "Gotta go. The camp starts in fifteen minutes." He mumbled something to Bailey about it being good to meet her.

"He's a nice kid," Bailey said, watching as Zach put on his helmet and rode away on his bike.

Nice certainly wasn't the word Parker would have used to describe him. Their relationship was strained at best. "I wasn't around much when he was growing up."

"Well, he certainly turned out all right." Bailey pulled back her shoulders, her attention still on the outside front. "People are starting to arrive."

Parker spotted three cars pulling into the parking lot. "You're sure you want to do business as usual?"

"I want to try." However, she didn't sound as certain as she had earlier. "I'll talk to my staff and the parents and tell them what's going on. If they want to keep their children away from here, then that's their decision, but I'll stay open for those who want to stay."

Parker took a deep breath, to gear up for round three with her, but he heard someone coming down the stairs. It was Sheriff Hale, and he was taking the steps two at a time.

"I just got a call," the sheriff told Parker. "That black car with the bogus plates that you saw on the surveillance tapes—my deputy just spotted it."

"Where?" Bailey immediately asked.

"On Main Street, just a few blocks away, and he's headed in this direction."

Chapter Three

Bailey paced across the reception area of the day care and checked the time on her cell phone. Five minutes since the last time she'd looked and over two hours since Sheriff Hale had told Parker and her about the black car.

Time was crawling by.

So was one of the toddlers, Bailey noticed.

She had to smile at the irony. Elijah, who was almost a year old, was trying to escape from the front playroom. He didn't get far before one of the workers, Audra Finmore, hurried out to scoop him up. Elijah giggled, obviously unaware of a menacing black car and her vandalized office.

"Any news?" Audra asked.

Bailey shook her head and checked her phone. Nothing other than the six calls from her mother, which she had let go straight to voice mail. Ditto for the two from her mother's personal bodyguard, Tim Penske, whom her mother had no doubt pestered to call Bailey, as well. But Bailey didn't want to talk to her mom or Tim until she had some answers, and right now she was very short of those.

She still wanted to believe this was nothing. Bailey wanted to stick with her bored-teenager theory to explain the slashed tires, the hang-up calls and the mess in her office. But until the sheriff spoke to the driver of that black car and got a reasonable explanation for why he was in town, then Bailey figured the knot in her stomach was there to stay.

"Enough of this," she mumbled.

The exteriors doors and windows were all locked, the security system was on and the sheriff would call the moment he knew anything. Since she couldn't use her office, Bailey decided to go to the playroom because she wanted the welcome distraction of the children.

First though, she stopped by the bathroom and touched up her makeup. There wasn't much she could do about her eyes that were red from crying, but she added some powder so that her cheeks wouldn't appear so streaked. She didn't want anyone to know that this situation had caused her to shed a single tear.

She strolled to the playroom where the staff and children were. There weren't many.

Two workers and seven children.

Normally, there would be six other staff members and close to fifty kids since parents from nearby towns brought their children to Cradles to Crayons. However, when Bailey had told everyone what was going on, only those with no other childcare choices left their children—even after she had assured them that she would do everything humanly possible to protect their children.

And she would. But it wouldn't bring back the children anytime soon.

It broke her heart.

This wasn't just her business. It was her life. And that idiot stalker was trying to rob her of what she loved most.

She fought back tears, again, and looked around the room. The tears dried up instantly when she spotted Parker. He was sitting on the floor, keeping watch out the front window where he'd pulled down the shade halfway.

But there was also a baby in his lap.

Maddie Simmons was almost two years old and had blond curls that haloed around her cherub cheeks. Unlike some of the other children, Maddie wasn't afraid of strangers.

Obviously.

She was right in Parker's face and was babbling while she wiggled her fingers in front of him. Parker continued to glance out the window, but his attention kept returning to Maddie.

Intrigued at this cowboy warrior's interaction with the angelic little girl, Bailey walked closer. Parker looked up, and their gazes collided. He had a strange expression on his face, a mixture of shock, concern, amusement and a little of get-me-out-of-here.

"She's teaching me the 'Itsy Bitsy Spider' song, I think," Parker explained.

Maddie verified that by smiling and babbling, "Bitty, bitty pider." She clapped her hands and then started another set of sounds. "Tinkle, tinkle."

Bailey recognized this one. "'Twinkle, Twinkle, Little Star.' I think she wants you to sing it."

Parker looked at Bailey as if she'd had just asked to jump out of plane without a parachute. "I don't think so. I can't sing."

That only encouraged Maddie to get closer. "Tinkle. Tinkle." She exaggerated the sounds as if trying to teach him.

Parker shook his head again, but Maddie persisted by pinching his mouth, and Parker finally mumbled the first line of the song. He was totally off-key, sounding very froglike, but it delighted Maddie so much that the little girl laughed and plopped a kiss on his cheek.

Despite the knot in her stomach, Bailey couldn't stave off a smile. Children were magical.

She walked closer and eased down on the floor beside them. She positioned herself so that she too could keep watch. "Anything from the sheriff?" she asked Parker.

"Fifteen minutes ago he called and said several deputies from the surrounding towns have joined the search."

"Good. If they're still looking, that means they still have hopes of finding the driver of that car."

"Maybe." Parker paused. "And what if they don't?"

That required a deep breath. "Then life goes on as usual." She glanced around at the handful of kids. "Or as close to usual as possible."

"Without me?" he pressed.

Another deep breath. "I'm sure with your credentials, Bart Bellows will have another job for you."

"We're back to that part about not wanting your mother to win."

"Yes," she said without hesitation. But then she hesitated. "You won't have trouble getting work elsewhere?"

"No," he also said without hesitation. "As soon as the sheriff gives us the all clear, I'll call Bart and tell him I'm off the case."

Bailey nodded. Good. This was what she wanted.

The knot in her stomach tightened.

Maddie tried to get up, but she got off balanced. Bailey reached for her, but Parker beat her to it. He gently caught onto the toddler's arm and steadied her.

"You're good with kids," she commented.

There it was again—the total shock in Parker's eyes. "I'm not."

Bailey flinched at his suddenly rough tone. "But Zach—"

"I wasn't around much when he was this age. Or any other age," he corrected.

That sounded like old baggage that he didn't especially want to discuss. Bailey shrugged. "I suppose it was hard for you to be home a lot because of your commitment to the army."

Parker didn't answer. He stared at the window, until Maddie began to sing her version of "Twinkle, Twinkle, Little Star." The cheerful song definitely didn't go with the somber mood in the room, but her staff was trying to keep things upbeat.

Charlotte was at a work table making Fourth of July decorations with two of the older children, and Audra was arranging the others into a circle for a scaled down version of Duck Duck Goose. Bailey knew from experience that all the running around from the game would tire out the kids, and at least several would need a nap.

When Maddie saw the game forming, she babbled bye-bye to Parker, gave him another kiss and toddled over to join the others.

"Why this?" Parker asked, drawing Bailey's attention back to him. "Why run a day care?" Parker's investigation had confirmed her trust fund. She didn't need to work. And she obviously loved kids…

Bailey heard the unspoken part of question, mainly because her mother often spoke it aloud. "You mean why am I here instead of raising a family of my own?"

Parker gave a begrudging nod. "I guess that's what I meant."

"I love kids, but I haven't met anyone I'd like to have kids with. My last relationship ended badly." Very badly. As in he turned out to be a low-life scum who cheated on her with a lap dancer and then told the press all about two-timing the governor's daughter. "Let's just say, I'm not a prize catch for most guys."

"Right." His eyebrow lifted. "You're beautiful, rich and smart. Guys hate that in a woman."

Bailey bit her lip to stop herself from smiling. "Thank you."

He thought she was beautiful.

That was something else to take her mind off the black car, but Bailey did glance out to make sure it wasn't there. "I also have a mother who's the governor, and while Mom says she would love for me to marry and give her grandchildren, she's yet to approve of any man I've dated."

Parker stared at her. "You need her approval?"

"No." Bailey pushed her hair away from her face. "But sometimes it would be nice to get it."

He made a sound, a rumble deep within his throat. "In the message that she left on your machine, she seemed to be playing matchmatcher with you and me."

"All talk, I assure you," Bailey mumbled. "She'll find fault even with a non-Neanderthal guy like you."

She hated this turn in the conversation. Hated that she'd just revealed something that personal to a man who was practically a stranger. If she continued with this, it wouldn't be long before she told him that she was toying with the idea of using artificial insemination to get pregnant.

Now, *that* would get him running. But it would also be revealing a secret wish that she wasn't ready to reveal to anyone. Time to switch gears to something more palatable, but Parker changed it for her.

"Who's that?" he asked and got to his feet.

She looked out the window and spotted the familiar dark-haired man making his way toward the porch. "Sidney Burrell, the handyman. He's putting in that bathroom Charlotte told you about." Bailey checked the date on her watch. "Though he wasn't supposed to work today. He only works after hours, after all the children are gone."

Parker stood at the window and studied him. "When he's here, he has access to the entire building?"

"Of course. Why?"

"You trust him?" Parker fired back.

Bailey was about to say yes, but she hesitated. "He moved to Freedom about four months ago so I don't know him that well, but he had good references. And he hasn't done anything to make me distrust him." She noticed his alarmed expression, and that alarmed her. "Why all the questions?"

Parker didn't take his attention off the man. "I think he's carrying a concealed weapon."

She jumped to her feet. "What?"

"Look at the slight bulge around the ankle of his jeans."

She did look, and yes, there was a bulge. "You think that means he has a gun?"

"Wait here," Parker ordered, and he hurried out the room and toward the front door.

Bailey had no intention of doing that. Ahead of her, Parker disengaged the security system and threw open the front door just as Sidney was coming up the steps. Even though Parker didn't draw his own gun, Sidney stopped in his tracks. His eyes widened, and he volleyed glances between Parker and her.

"I heard about the car everyone's looking for," Sidney said. "It's all over town. I came over to check on you."

"I'm fine," Bailey lied.

Parker stepped out onto the porch and would have shut the door in her face, if she hadn't caught onto it. Parker shot her a warning glance over his shoulder, probably so that she would go back inside, but Bailey went on the porch with him.

"This is Parker McKenna," she said, trying to make it sound like a casual introduction.

Parker didn't wait for Sidney to respond. "Are you carrying a gun?"

Sidney pulled back his shoulders. "What business is that of yours?"

"Are you carrying a gun?" Parker repeated. He took a single step closer to Sidney, but that step along with his expression had a menacing feel to it.

"Yeah." Sidney's expression took on a menacing feel, as well. "I am. But I have a permit to carry concealed."

Since Bailey's emotions were already running high, she forced herself to put this in perspective, though she didn't like the fact this man had been in her day care with a weapon strapped to his ankle.

Except Parker had a weapon too, she reminded herself.

"Why carry a gun?" Bailey asked.

Sidney shrugged and softened his glare when he looked at her. "My house isn't in town, and a time or two I've come home to find coyotes in my yard. It's easier to have the gun on me than in the glove compartment of the truck."

She nodded, accepting that. "I'd prefer if you didn't wear it in the building," she simply stated.

Sidney's mouth tightened. "If that's the way you want it."

"It is," Parker answered for her.

For a moment she thought Sidney might argue with that, but he finally smiled and tipped his fingers to his forehead in a mock salute. "I'll be seeing you around."

For some reason, that sounded like a threat. Or maybe it was just the nerves getting to her. Parker and she stood there and watched Sidney walk away. The man got into a blue pickup truck and drove off.

"You should call Bart and ask him to run a background check on this guy," Parker suggested.

That was a good idea, and Bailey made a mental note to be more careful about the people she hired. When had her life gotten so complicated?

Her phone rang, and even though she'd been expecting and even praying for this particular call, her heart began to pound when she saw the sheriff's name on the screen. Her hand was shaking too, but she pressed the button to answer it and put it on speaker so Parker could hear.

"Did you find the car?" Bailey immediately asked.

"No," Sheriff Hale said after several snail-crawling moments. "We looked hard, Bailey, but that car isn't on any road in this county. I figure the guy knows we're onto him, and he's long gone."

Bailey tried not to react, and on the outside she probably didn't. Inside was a different matter.

"We'll keep looking, of course," the sheriff continued. "I'll review each new security tape. And I'll have one of the deputies drive by Cradles to Crayons at least every hour. We got this situation under control, Bailey, and I don't want you worrying about it."

"Thank you," she told him, and she clicked the end call button.

She didn't move. Bailey just stood there, even though the July heat was brutal. Sweat was starting to trickle down her back.

"Okay," Parker mumbled. "That's that, then." He extended his hand for her to shake.

A farewell shake, no doubt.

Bailey stared at his hand. Then at Parker himself. And she had the sickening feeling that her life depended on the decision she was about to make.

Chapter Four

Well, it was a victory, but Parker didn't feel like celebrating.

Yes, Bailey had told him that he could continue to be her bodyguard, but since she'd snarled when she said it, Parker didn't think this was an employer-employee match made in heaven.

She drove ahead of him in her BMW and pulled into her neighborhood, an area Parker knew well since he'd been watching her for days.

But who else had been watching her?

Parker had been careful and observant, and he hadn't seen anyone suspicious, but those surveillance tapes proved otherwise. He hoped like hell that the driver of that mysterious black car didn't have some kind of insider information about Bailey's schedule, but then she was pretty predictable.

During the workweek, Bailey went to the day care at six forty-five and came home around seven p.m. Sometimes later. She often took meals with female friends or members of her staff at the diner, Talk of the Town, but other than that, she didn't have much of a social life.

Was that because she was nursing a broken heart?

Since Parker had already done an extensive background check on Bailey, he knew about her failed relationship with the Dallas real estate tycoon Trey Masters, who'd been downright chatty with the tabloids about what it was like to date the governor's daughter. It hadn't been pretty, and since that happened only four months ago, that might explain the no-male company in Bailey's life.

Parker also knew other things. Personal things. For instance, on Saturday, Bailey had visited a fertility clinic in Amarillo. He knew because he'd followed her there and had seen her collect their literature on artificial insemination and single parenthood. He wondered if the governor knew about her daughter's possible plans to become a mother.

Having a child of her own would suit Bailey all right. He had seen her with the children at the day care, and she was a natural.

Ahead of him, Bailey pulled into the driveway of her prairie-style house. It was homey, not at all what he'd expected when he'd first seen it a week earlier. Across the entire front of the house was a porch, complete with hanging plants, rocking chairs and even a swing.

She got out and immediately looked back at him as he brought his truck to a stop behind her. Even though she was wearing dark sunglasses now, she was no doubt still glaring. And probably hating that she had no other choice but to rely on him for her personal safety.

"There's no reason for you to check the house," she told him, again.

Parker ignored her, *again*. "I just want to make sure no one has broken in."

"I have a security system, and I use it."

"So you've said. But there are ways around a security system. Humor me, Bailey. This won't take long, and it'll make me sleep better tonight."

She huffed, just as he knew she would do, and pushed her shades to the top of her head. With her keys ready, she walked to front door. Probably because her hands were still shaking, something she wouldn't dare admit, it took her several seconds to get it unlocked. Almost immediately the security system began to whine, and she punched in the code on the wall keypad to disarm it.

"Wait right here," Parker insisted. And in this case, *right here* was just inside the doorway. He didn't want her outside alone, but he didn't want her in the house itself until he gave the all-clear.

He stepped around her, their shoulders brushing. Not good. Even that small amount of contact caused him to remember that in addition to being the job, Bailey was an attractive woman that got his body humming.

Parker told his body to knock it off.

He drew his gun and got to work, making his way through the living room and into the kitchen. He figured there'd be high-end furnishings and decor, maybe black granite countertops, lots of crystal and mirrored stainless appliances, but it was more old-fashioned than newfangled. Butcher-block counters and whitewashed cabinets. There was a jar of crunchy peanut butter and a loaf of bread on the center island.

The word that came to mind was *cozy.*

Bailey lived a lot more normal life than he'd expected. She certainly didn't live like the daughter of a governor with roots that were Texas royalty.

From the kitchen Parker went through the dining room and checked the laundry room before he went to the side of the house with the bedrooms. There were three of them, all decorated in that same cozy style with warm colored walls and quilts on the beds.

He instantly knew which bedroom was Bailey's because it still carried her scent. He glanced at the bed, unmade, with the sugar-white covers rumpled as if she'd just gotten up. For just a flash of an instant, he got an image of her climbing, naked, from that bed.

Hell.

He didn't need that image in his head.

"See anything?" Bailey asked.

Parker nearly jumped out of his skin. She was right behind him, and he had no idea how that'd happened. Oh, yeah. He did. He'd been caught up in that whole *naked, sugar-white sheets* fantasy and was fighting the effects that both the fantasy and the woman had on his body.

He shot her a scowl about breaking his stay-put rule and checked the adjoining bathroom. No one was there. But there was a claw-footed tub with a stack of paperbacks and several bottles of bubble bath beside it.

Again, he got the naked image, this time with sudsy water sliding down her—

"Everything looks just as I left it," she commented, snapping him back. "No bogeymen. Plus, it's still daylight, and my neighbors have no doubt heard about the office incident and the black car. They'll be on the lookout, so I seriously doubt a stranger will make it within a hundred yards of my place without one of the neighbors calling me and Sheriff Hale."

That's what Parker was hoping.

He was also hoping his body would soften.

Parker reholstered his gun and waited until Bailey was out of the doorway before he walked past her. No more accidental touching. He had enough going on inside him without adding the real thing.

"Lock the door when I leave," he instructed. "And set the security alarm. I already gave you my number, and if you have to go out for any reason, call me. I'll come over and go with you. Oh, I'll be back tomorrow morning to drive you to work."

She wearily shook her head and followed him to the door. "We'll be joined at the hip."

Man. That sounded sexual, too. "Until this guy is caught, yes."

"Am I allowed to say that I hate having to rely on you for peace of mind?" she asked.

Parker smiled before he could stop himself. "You're allowed." He made the mistake of looking at her. Really looking. And he saw the strain of all of this deep in those jeweled blue eyes. "Am I allowed to say that I'm sorry this is happening to you?"

"No." But then she smiled, too. It was brief and filled with as much weariness as was in her eyes. "I'm not big on people feeling sorry for me."

That wasn't exactly a surprise. "Or leaning on anyone," Parker supplied.

His comment brought her eyes back to his. "That, too." She swallowed hard. "I just want my life back."

Everything inside him said this was a good time to leave. Give Bailey a pat on the arm, say something reassuring and then get the heck out of there. Being around her was like playing with an inferno.

But Parker didn't do as his insides told him.

He went with a different part of his body, and that would have been all right, maybe, if his thoughts had been purely sexual and in search of the cheap thrill of holding her in his arms. But his heart got in on this, too.

Parker hated to see her hurting like this.

Yes, she was a stubborn pain in the butt, but she was also a vulnerable woman. He was a sucker for a damsel in distress, and while Bailey wasn't exactly a damsel, she did have that distress part whether she wanted it or not.

Cursing himself, he reached out and slipped his hand around her waist. One nudge, and Parker did indeed get Bailey in his arms. She went right into them as if she belonged there, and the embrace put them body to body again.

His heart might have been what prompted him to comfort her, but his runaway imagination soon got in on the deal. Parker thought of her bed again. Her, naked. Him, naked and in that bed with her. Those long, beautiful, athletic legs wrapped around him while he did exactly what his body was begging him to do.

Mercy.

When his assignment was over, he really did need to take the time to be with a woman.

Her warm breath hit against his neck. Almost like a kiss, and his imagination filled in the blanks. Her breathing also created some interesting contact with her breasts against his chest. She didn't put her arms around him. Didn't need to. There was already too much contact as it was.

"Don't read anything into this," she mumbled. "You just caught me in a weak moment, that's all."

That cut right through the scalding-hot fantasy, and Parker pulled back so he could meet her gaze. "You're allowed weak moments."

She frowned, caught onto his arm to move him away. But then looked down at his biceps. "I think your muscles have muscles," she mumbled.

Parker nearly laughed. "I'm not that big."

Her left eyebrow slid up, and she smiled without actually smiling. Parker wasn't sure who blushed more—Bailey or him. Thankfully, the humiliation was cut short when the black limo pulled into Bailey's driveway next to his truck.

Bailey stepped away from him but not before cursing under her breath. "That's my mother."

Parker was already going for his gun, but that stopped him. "You were expecting her?"

"Not a chance. I would have warned you. Brace yourself. She probably saw the way we were standing, and she'll read a lot into it. Prepare yourself for questions that have nothing to do with being my bodyguard."

Great. Just what he needed when every part of him below the belt was still humming with those naked images of Bailey.

A bulky thirty-something man with chestnut hair got out first. He was built like a wrestler. No neck and wide shoulders. He shot Bailey and Parker a look, and even though he was across the lawn from them, Parker thought he sensed some disapproval.

"That's Tim Penske," Bailey provided. "He's my mother's bodyguard. Very intense guy. Very bodyguard-ish. I think his muscles have muscles, too."

Parker ignored the inside joke and watched as Tim watched back. The man didn't take his eyes off them when he walked to one of the passenger doors and opened it.

"He's worked for your mother a long time?" Parker questioned.

"All seven years that she's been governor." She glanced at Parker and probably noticed the way he was studying Tim. "Why do you ask?"

Parker shook his head. Best to keep his gut feelings to himself, but it seemed as if Tim Penske took an instant dislike to him.

Governor Lila Lockhart stepped from the limo, her gaze going straight to her daughter and then to Parker. No instant dislike here. She gave them a brief smile and started toward them. Her hair was blond, like Bailey's, but was cut short. She was shorter as well, at least five inches shorter than her daughter. The woman wore a perfectly tailored sky-blue shirt suit with matching heels.

Tim was behind her.

Lila's smile faded as she approached the door. "You didn't answer my calls," she said to Bailey. "So, despite dinner plans that I had to cancel at the last minute, I came to check on you."

"No need." Bailey straightened her shoulders. "As you can see, the non-Neanderthal bodyguard that you secretly hired is right here. Just as you wanted."

"Just as *you needed,*" Lila corrected. Lila extended her hand to Parker for him to shake. "I apologize if my daughter is giving you a hard time."

Oh, Bailey was doing that, in more than one sense of the word.

"This is my own bodyguard, Tim Penske. I'm not above relying on someone for personal protection." Lila lifted her hand toward the man, and her shift in position caused the setting sun to catch the facets in her diamond cross necklace around her neck. "Tim, this is Captain McKenna."

"Parker," he offered, though he certainly didn't see anything friendly in his fellow bodyguard's eyes.

"Any word on the car the sheriff is looking for?" Tim asked, sounding all business. He also glanced around the yard as if he expected someone might jump out and attack.

"No," Parker and Bailey said in unison, and their gazes connected again. Unlike Tim, Bailey seemed to be bracing herself for another kind of battle. Maybe with her mother? He knew Bailey was still riled about this whole bodyguard thing.

"Let's go inside," Lila said, catching onto Bailey's

arm. "We need to talk. Apparently, I have to eat some crow to get back in your good graces."

"Want me to stay?" Parker asked her.

Bailey shook her head. "Go home to Zach. Basketball camp's over by now, and he'll probably be wondering where you are."

With everything else going on, Parker was surprised she would remember the basketball camp. "Lock up when your mother leaves," Parker reminded her.

"It was good meeting you," Lila told him.

"Good meeting you, too." And he headed out the door and toward his truck.

Tim followed him.

Apparently, the man had something to say, and Parker welcomed it. He wanted an explanation as to why Tim was staring holes in him. Parker didn't have to wait long.

"I thought you should know that I objected when Governor Lockhart said she was going to hire you," Tim said. "I told her she should get someone with more experience."

Parker just stared back at him. "I did combat bodyguard duty. I have plenty of experience."

"Maybe with army types, but Bailey isn't in the army, and this isn't a combat field, *Captain* McKenna." The muscles in Tim's face were so tight Parker thought he could have bounced a quarter off them.

Parker decided to test a theory. "You're sure this objection isn't more personal?"

There. Parker saw it. Tim flinched just a little but enough for Parker to know he'd hit a nerve.

"What do you mean? Did Bailey tell you that? Did she say something?" Tim didn't even draw breath during those rapid-fire questions.

"About you?" Parker didn't wait for an answer. He just shrugged. "Bailey said nothing, other than you work for her mother."

Another slight flinch. Oh, yeah. There was something beneath the surface of Tim's stony expression. Feelings for Bailey maybe.

Maybe something more.

"You want to talk about what Bailey said, or do you have something else on your mind?" Parker demanded.

Tim had to get his teeth unclenched before he could speak. "My only concern is Bailey and her mother. That means *you* concern me. Have you made any progress whatsoever in finding out who's doing these things to Bailey?"

"Some." Parker debated how much he should say, but he couldn't let his dislike for this guy hurt the investigation. Besides, Lila would soon know everything, and she would probably tell Tim. "Bailey's handyman, Sidney Burrell, stopped by Cradles to Crayons today. He was carrying a concealed weapon. I verified that he does have a permit, but I want to run a background check on him."

Tim whipped out a phone from his pocket and punched in some numbers. "Sidney Burrell," he said to whoever answered. "What can you find out about him?" Tim slipped his hand over the receiver. "The governor's personal assistant is running a computer check," he let Parker know.

Parker expected to have to endure a long wait, but it was only a few seconds.

"He's twenty-three," Tim relayed. "Went to elementary school here in Freedom, but his family moved to a nearby town when he was ten. He has a gun permit and a hunting license. Rents property on one of the farms roads outside city limits."

All benign stuff, and it meshed with what Sidney had told him. But then Tim's eyes widened a little. "What's the name of the judge?" Tim asked.

Judge?

Hell. This probably wasn't going to be good news.

Tim's eyes widened even more, and he snapped the phone shut. "Sidney Burrell has a sealed juvenile record."

Parker had braced himself for something worse. "That's it?"

"Maybe. But I'm guessing there's more. He went up in front of Judge Elmore Thompson, and he wouldn't have been in that court if he hadn't done something serious."

"How serious?" Parker repeated.

"Probably something violent. It's definitely something he wants hidden because over the past four months, Sidney Burrell has been trying to have it expunged."

Four months. When he started working for Bailey.

Parker didn't like the timing.

"I'll call Corps Security and Investigations," Parker

insisted. "I want that sealed record unsealed. Sidney Burrell has secrets, and I want to know exactly what they are."

Chapter Five

Bailey heard the laughter. It traveled all the way up the stairs and to her office. That wasn't unusual. She often kept her door open just so she could hear the sounds of the children. But today she heard a different laughter.

Parker's.

His voice certainly stood out among her female-only staff and the children.

From the sound of it, he was playing games with the day-care kids. And everyone was having fun. Bailey didn't begrudge that fun. After all, she'd been the one to insist that Parker not stay right next to her. She had shooed him away when he had tried to help her clean her office.

She checked her watch. That had been four hours ago. Time apparently flew by when there was a vandalized mess to clean, but it was all finally done. So was the constant stream of daily paperwork needed to run a business. However, she was hungry now. Since Parker had shown up at her house fifteen minutes before she was due to leave, and because the sight of him had disrupted her, Bailey had forgotten to pack a lunch.

Following the sound of the laughter, she grabbed her purse and made her way down the stairs and across the reception area. She found Parker in the large playroom. He wasn't standing guard at the window, probably because he'd made sure all the doors and windows were locked and that the security system was turned on. With those measures taken, he was building a block house with Maddie and several of the other toddlers.

Bailey stood there a moment just watching them. Or rather watching *Parker.* For lack of a better word, he looked perfect in his butt-hugging jeans and gray shirt that clung to every one of those toned muscles.

He was sizzling.

There was no denying that, and despite the fact that Bailey had decided to resist him at all costs, seeing him like this was really wearing down her resistance.

Parker looked up, snagged her gaze and smiled. He was hot with his usual somber semiscowl, but he was something well beyond hot with that meet-me in-the-bedroom smile. She was so glad he couldn't read her mind.

Maddie tried to pick up one of the blocks and nearly tumbled headfirst into the house. Parker saved the moment by scooping her up. Maddie laughed when Parker goosed her in the belly.

"Daddy Corps to the rescue," Bailey joked.

"Sounds a little less intimating than Corps Security and Investigations, huh?" Parker eased Maddie on the floor, got to his feet and walked to Bailey. "Going somewhere?" He tipped his head to the purse that she had tucked under her arm.

"I'm headed across the street to the café for some lunch."

He waved goodbye to Maddie and the others. "I'll come with you."

Bailey had expected him to say exactly that, and even though she was still riled at her loss of freedom, she was getting used to the idea of having Parker around.

Now, if she could stop drooling whenever she looked at him.

"How did the visit go with your mother?" he asked as they made their way out of the building. Parker stayed close and looked around, no doubt for that black car or anything else that was sinister.

Bailey looked, too, and then put on her sunglasses that she took from her purse. "Her visit was like most of her visits. We argued first about her hiring you, and then we argued about arguing." There was also a good bit of conversation where her mother emphasized Parker's drool-worthiness, but Bailey kept that to herself.

"I was surprised she was in the area," Parker commented. "I thought she'd be in Austin at the governor's mansion."

"She's at Twin Harts, our family ranch," she added in case he hadn't heard. The muggy July breeze swiped at her hair, sending it into her face. "It's her sanctuary and where she always goes when she's mulling something over."

"Like running for president?"

Bailey nodded, not surprised that Parker knew. Her mother's life was pretty much an open book. "But I think she also wants to keep an eye on me."

Her mind was on exactly that when Bailey started to cross the street. She glanced around, but she didn't see the white Ford Focus that would have mowed her down if Parker hadn't caught onto her arm the way he'd caught onto Maddie just minutes earlier.

"Sorry!" the driver called out to her. That was polite since Bailey had been at fault.

"Thanks," she mumbled to Parker.

"Something other than the obvious bothering you?" he questioned. He kept hold of her arm as they crossed the street, and they started the short trek to the Talk of the Town café.

Since he was touching her, she tried not to stiffen or have another visible reaction. She certainly didn't want to discuss the little hugging session in the doorway that her mother had witnessed.

"I was thinking about Tim, my mother's bodyguard." And she was, sort of. She had thought about Tim in those moments when she hadn't succeeded in getting her mind off her own hot bodyguard.

She felt Parker's hand stiffen slightly, and she glanced at him, unsure of what had caused his scowl to return. "What did Tim and you discuss before you left my house last night?" Bailey asked.

Parker did another sweeping look around them. No one was nearby. "I asked him about Sidney Burrell. Your handyman has a sealed juvenile record that I'm trying to get unsealed. Whatever Sidney did, it's serious. Probably something violent."

Oh, no.

Bailey shook her head. She didn't need this on top of

everything else. She wanted to give Sidney the benefit of the doubt, but her life was too crazy now to blindly trust anyone.

"I'll call him," she said, "and tell that his services are no longer needed."

"I already have."

Bailey was in midreach for the café door, but that had her freezing. "You did what?"

Parker huffed, obviously noting her displeasure. "All I said was that you wouldn't need him for a while because the bathroom renovations had to be put on hold. You'll thank me for it later."

She whipped off her sunglasses so he could see the glare she aimed at him. "Maybe. But for right now, I'm just a little upset that I wasn't given the opportunity to do it myself. I'm not an idiot or incompetent, Parker."

And since she said that louder than she'd planned, the people inside the café turned to stare.

"If I hadn't called Sidney, Tim would have, and he would have been a lot less tactful," Parker explained, his voice much lower than hers. "In fact, he wanted the sheriff to pick up Sidney for questioning. I talked him out of that. Best not to antagonize a possible stalking suspect unless we have some proof that he's actually done anything wrong."

"Great. Now I have Tim trying to control my life." Since everyone seemed to be trying to hear their conversation, Bailey threw open the door.

"Bailey," the strawberry-blonde behind the cash registry greeted. It was Faith Scott, the owner of Talk of the Town. "Your usual booth is waiting for you."

"Thanks." Bailey didn't miss the inquisitive smile Faith was giving Parker. All the other diners had their eyes on him, too, so Bailey went for a group introduction. "This is Parker McKenna, my bodyguard. Yes, I did say *bodyguard*."

She braced herself for some ribbing, maybe a comment or two about Parker being her mother's latest matchmaking attempt. But nothing. Just a few head bobs and mumbles of agreement from the regulars.

Not good.

Did everyone in town think she was on the verge of being killed by her office-trashing stalker?

Her mother's life might be an open book, but Bailey valued her privacy too much to be happy about being the subject of the town's gossips.

Faith, who was mega pregnant, followed Parker and her across the room to her usual spot. Everything about the café was homey and welcoming, but Bailey preferred the booth because she could still see the day care. She trusted her staff and enjoyed her lunches at the diner, but there was just something comforting about seeing the business she'd built from the ground up.

"The special today is meat loaf. My grandmother's recipe," Faith explained, looking at Parker. "But I'm guessing you're more of a steak-and-potatoes guy?"

"The meat loaf sounds good," he assured her. "I'll take a glass of iced tea to go with it."

Faith smiled, obviously approving. Parker clearly wasn't going to have any trouble wooing Freedom.

Bailey ordered the same and waited for Faith to step away before she continued Parker's and her conversation.

"What else did Tim and you come up with in that little chat in my driveway?"

She expected a quick comeback, maybe a dismissal that they'd discussed anything else. But Parker took a deep breath and stared at her. "How do you feel about Tim?"

The question threw her, and she studied him trying to figure out where this was going. "I don't feel much at all about him. Why?"

"Have you ever dated him?"

"No." She couldn't say that fast enough. "Tim had a thing for me when he first started working for my mother. He asked me out. Called me a few times. But I told him I wasn't interested. He's not my type."

The corner of Parker's mouth lifted for just a second. "Too many muscles?" he joked.

"Too intense." She paused and ducked down her head a little to keep the eye contact when Parker shifted position. "Why? Did he say something to you?"

"It's more what he didn't say." He shrugged. "But I'm guessing your mother had him thoroughly checked out before she hired him."

"I'm sure she did." Or she should have. Bailey made a mental note to find out.

"Two meat loaf specials, two teas," Faith said, delivering their meal. The plates were filled to the edges with not just the meat loaf but mashed potatoes, gravy and green beans. "And I've got peanut-butter brownies fresh from the oven."

Faith knew she wouldn't be able to resist. Peanut butter was her weakness. "Wrap me up one to go,"

Bailey told her. "It'll be my afternoon snack." And the reason she'd have to spend extra time on the treadmill tonight.

"Better make that two brownies, Faith," Stan Lorry, the diner at the counter, called out. He was in his sixties and built like Santa Claus, but there was obviously nothing wrong with his hearing. "I'm betting Bailey's bodyguard will want a nibble or two, as well."

That caused laughter to ripple through the room, and Bailey hated that she felt herself blush. Sheesh. Was nothing off-limits?

"Some people just like to gossip," Faith mumbled and strolled away.

"Yeah," the young waitress, Molly Allen, agreed. "And most of those *some people* are sitting right here in this café." Molly aimed her pointing finger right over Stan's head and then moved that pointing finger onto Mabel Watson, a retired seventy-something bar owner and Francine Determeyer, her eccentric friend who wore hot-pink spandex pants and rhinestone flip-flops.

More laughter. Molly continued with her finger pointing joke.

"Sorry about this," Bailey mumbled. "Tomorrow, I'll pack a lunch."

"No. It's all right. You needed to get out of that office." Parker took a bite of his meat loaf, and made a *mmmm* sound, but his attention was on the other diners. "Is it always crowded like this?"

"Always. Faith serves up good food, and it's a place for people to come, hang out with friends, and...gossip," she settled for saying.

"How about strangers? You get many of those in the café?"

Bailey nodded. "Sure." She tipped her head to the couple in the first booth. "Never seen them before, but Freedom is a stopover for people on road trips headed to Amarillo. A lot of the temporary-hire ranch hands drop by, too."

Parker glanced around again. "I need to tell Bart Bellows about this. I think it's a good idea to have someone work surveillance here. With all the gossip, there might be talk about who could be responsible for the threats against your mother and you."

It was a good idea, and Bailey wished she had thought of it. The letters that her mother had been getting might turn out to be nothing, but in light of what was going on in Bailey's own life, she couldn't be sure. The same person who was tormenting her could be responsible for those letters.

She and Parker tried to ignore the whispers about them that were going around the diner. Mabel apparently thought they were sleeping together. Bailey hoped Parker hadn't heard that, but one glance at his face let her know that he had.

He had a knack for smiling without smiling. A sort of sly thing he did with his perfectly shaped mouth. "Well, I did come close to kissing you last night," he murmured.

Yes, he had. Bailey had dreamed about it. She'd also dreamed he'd succeeded, that the kiss had happened and her mother and Tim had never shown up to interrupt them.

"This attraction could turn out to be a problem." Parker looked at her from over the top of his iced-tea glass.

Bailey hated the bluntness because now she had to address it. She hated even more that it was true. "If I kiss you, my mother will win," she said, only partly joking.

For a moment she thought he was going to continue the little teasing session going on. All the eye contact. The subtle looks. The heat stirring around them. But he didn't. Parker's expression shifted, and he was the stern warrior again.

"My job is to protect you," he said. It sounded as if he were talking to himself.

"Plus, there's Zach." She didn't exactly pull it out of thin air, but Bailey thought it might be a good idea to remind herself there were obstacles other than her mother. "He's had a lot of upheavals recently what with the move and switching schools. He doesn't need you spending more time or energy on me."

Parker made a sound of disagreement, which he didn't explain. Instead, his gaze shot right past her. To the window.

"Sidney Burrell," he spat out.

Bailey looked up and saw the man making his way across the front lawn of the day care. Oh, mercy. She didn't want him near the children, not until she had more information about his background.

Parker got up, and in the same motion he took out his wallet and dropped some money on the table. "We'll have to come back for that brownie," he said to Faith who was clearly startled at their hasty exit.

"You should wait here," he said to Bailey. "But since I know you won't, will you at least stay behind me?"

"I doubt Sidney will do anything crazy in broad daylight on Main Street," she argued.

Parker glared at her.

"But yes, I'll stay behind you," she finally conceded.

Sidney saw them coming because he stopped right at the base of the porch steps and waited. Over the past four months, Bailey had seen him several dozen times, but she had never seen him like this. He'd always shown up to work well groomed and with a pleasant expression, but his expression was anything but pleasant now.

"Ms. Lockhart." It wasn't a greeting, more like profanity, and that attitude didn't improve when Sidney's gaze landed on Parker. "I came to talk to Ms. Lockhart *alone*."

"That's not going to happen," Parker assured him. "Whatever you have to say to her, you can say in front of me."

Bailey glanced at the windows of the day care and was relieved that none of the children or her staff were looking outside. She didn't think this encounter would turn violent, but she didn't want them witnessing something that could be upsetting.

She was almost certain this would qualify as *upsetting.*

Sidney nailed his attention to Parker. "Ms. Lockhart's the one who hired me, not you, not her mother's bodyguard either, and I want to hear from her own lips why I'm no longer good enough to work for her."

So Tim had contacted Sidney after all. That did not please her.

"It's because of your juvenile record," Bailey admitted. She stepped to Parker's side, earning her another glare from Parker, but she ignored it and him. Maybe, just maybe, she could defuse this situation and Sidney's anger.

"That record was sealed," Sidney snapped.

"Yes, but the judge who sealed it only presided over cases of a violent nature," Parker snapped right back.

Something went through Sidney's eyes. Not exactly surprise but something else. It was almost as if he were embarrassed. Humble, even.

"It was a misunderstanding with an old girlfriend," he explained, shaking his head. "We got drunk at a party, and when some guy hit on her, I got into a fight and broke the guy's nose. That was eight years ago when I was fifteen and stupid. And that's all there was to it."

"No," Parker said almost immediately. "That's not all there is to it."

That wiped out any shred of humbleness. Sidney's eyes were already dark, but they darkened even more. "You SOB. You got the records unsealed."

Parker hadn't, he'd already let her know that, but he didn't admit it to Sidney. "I know what you did, and I don't want you around Bailey or the children."

Sidney mumbled some vicious profanity. The muscles in his jaw turned to iron. "This isn't over," he threatened.

Parker reached out, grabbed onto a handful of Sidney's shirt and snapped him closer. "Yes. It is."

Sidney might have been ready to burst with anger, but he slid his gaze over Parker, who was much bigger. Much stronger. And Sidney must have known this wasn't a battle he could win.

Not at this moment anyway.

Sidney looked right at her, those eyes on fire with not just anger but with rage. "I'll be seeing you around, Ms. Lockhart."

And with that, he turned and stormed away.

Bailey just stood there, watching him leave, and knowing in her heart that she hadn't seen the last of him. For the first time since all of this had started, Bailey felt something she didn't feel.

Fear.

Not for herself but the children under her care.

"I have to do something," Bailey managed to say. She hurried up the steps. She had to get to her office now.

Chapter Six

Time was up, and Parker started up the stairs to Bailey's office. He needed to check on her and make sure she wasn't doing something they would both regret. Besides, he had some news, and this particular news wouldn't keep, even if it was going to add to her already stressful situation.

After the ugly encounter with Sidney Burrell, she'd asked for an hour alone in her office. *To compose herself,* she'd mumbled to Parker when he'd ask what she planned to do. But Parker hadn't seen just fear on Bailey's face, he'd seen a Texas-size dose of anger, too. Sometimes anger could be a good thing, but he wasn't sure that was the case here.

Her office door was closed, and Parker knocked once and opened it. She had her elbows on her desk, her face buried in her hands. She looked up, their gazes colliding, and Parker saw then that she'd been crying.

"I'm still composing myself," she snapped.

In other words, she wanted him to leave her alone. But Parker didn't do that. He stepped inside, shut the door behind him and went to her.

"You called Tim?" he asked, but he already knew the answer. Bailey had phoned the man and had probably blasted him big-time for contacting Sidney Burrell.

"Tim said he was only looking out for me." She drew in a long breath and leaned back in her chair. "I feel as if I'm in kindergarten and can't tie my own shoes."

"Did you yell at him?" Parker tried to keep his tone light, but there was nothing light inside him. There was a fierce storm, and he hated that Bailey had all these other pressures in addition to a stalker. A stalker who might or might not be the handyman who'd just confronted and threatened her.

"I did some yelling," she admitted. "I think I clarified that I don't need or want Tim interfering in my life. Besides, I'm sure he's reporting every little detail to my mother, and she already has enough on her mind."

Yes. Because Lila Lockhart was receiving her own threats. But they were nothing compared to Bailey's. Lila's had been confined to some vaguely worded letters, none of which had threatened her safety or her life, but Parker was reasonably sure Sidney had done that to Bailey just an hour ago.

"I have to shut down Cradles to Crayons," Bailey whispered.

That explained the tears. Bailey could deal with Tim's interference, Sidney's threats and even the vandalized office.

But closing this place was like a cut to her heart.

"I've been calling parents," she continued, her voice clogged with emotion. She had to blink back more tears. "I asked them to make other arrangements for child care until this situation is resolved." She looked up at him. "Please tell me it'll be resolved soon."

"It will be," he promised, and that was a promise Parker would keep. He didn't want Bailey put through any more of this, and there might finally be some light at the end of this particular tunnel.

"Bart Bellows managed to get Sidney's record unsealed," Parker told her.

Her eyes widened, and she slowly got to her feet. "It's bad?"

"Yeah," Parker confirmed. "Sidney told the truth about getting drunk and the fight with the kid who hit on his girlfriend. But what he failed to mention was that he also assaulted his girlfriend. The attack was serious enough to put her in the hospital."

"Oh, mercy." Since she looked ready to drop back in the chair, Parker slid his arm around her waist.

"There's more." And this was the part he hated to tell her, but it was also the part that might put an end to this. "After his girlfriend was released from the hospital, Sidney stalked her. He slashed the tires on her mother's car and vandalized her house. He spent a year in juvenile hall."

Her eyes widened, and she shook her head. "And this is the man I hired."

"You couldn't have known about the juvenile file. Even if you'd run a thorough background check, it wouldn't have automatically popped up. Plus, he's had a clean record since."

"Or maybe he just hasn't been caught doing anything illegal," Bailey suggested.

"It's possible, and that's the reason Sheriff Hale will have a deputy tailing Sidney. Bart is sending out someone, as well. If Sidney makes one wrong move, then he'll be arrested."

Bailey paused a moment. "Good," she whispered. And then she repeated it. "But why come after me like this? I'm obviously not his girlfriend, and he hasn't made any sexual advances toward me."

Parker shrugged. "Who knows. He might have interpreted a simple friendly gesture as a come-on and another simple gesture as a rejection. It's possible he's not mentally stable."

She groaned. "Great. I might have placed the children in danger by hiring a psychopath."

"This isn't your fault," he reminded her.

But Bailey shook her head and tried to shake off his grip, too. Parker held on, and when the tears threatened again, he pulled her into his arms.

She looked up at him at the same moment he looked down at her. Bailey blinked at those tears again, but she did something else. Her tongue flicked over her bottom lip. It meant nothing, he assured himself. Her lips were dry, that was all. She needed some ChapStick and not a kiss. But to his suddenly revved-up body, that little gesture seemed like a big invitation.

Bailey didn't take her eyes off him. Didn't blink. Didn't move. But something changed.

Oh, yeah.

His own body changed, that's for sure. It started to harden in places it shouldn't, and despite that, Parker began to ease her closer.

He leaned down. She came up on her toes. They were moving in on each other.

Obviously, both of them had lots their minds.

Bailey could at least blame her mind loss on the danger, but Parker had no excuse. None. All he knew was that his need to protect her hadn't gotten all mixed up with this other need. The need that caused an ache in his entire body. And it was that ache that made him want to taste her more than he wanted to hang on to his sanity.

The first touch of his mouth to hers was a jolt.

Like lightning, except this was pure pleasure. Bailey tasted like birthday cake, Christmas and Fourth of July all rolled into one.

She made a sound deep in her throat that let him know this was pleasurable for her, too. She lifted her left arm, slid it around his neck and then did the same with her right, all the while nudging him closer.

Parker got closer, all right. He snapped her to him and kissed her the hard way. The way that would make it impossible for him to ever look at her again and not think of this.

And that wasn't good.

He was her bodyguard. He needed to stay objective, focused, and French kissing her didn't fall into the objective or focused categories.

Parker ordered himself to stop.

That didn't work.

Bailey tightened the grip she had on him and did her own part to deepen the kiss. Her body pressed against his, perfectly fitting pieces of a puzzle, with her breasts against his chest. Her stomach against his.

And other parts, too.

This wasn't a kiss. It was foreplay.

Parker put his hand between them just to give them a little space, and he forced himself to stop the French part of the kissing. What he didn't do was move back, and there was still a lot of him touching a lot of her.

"I thought we agreed this wouldn't be a good idea," Bailey whispered.

"It's not," Parker concurred. Not easily. Hell, simple speech wasn't easy for him right now.

And walking away would be impossible.

"So why can't we stop?" she asked.

"Because we're stupid when it comes to each other."

She smiled, and he felt the smile on his own lips. He wanted to taste that smile. Wanted to taste every inch of her. But what he really needed was a cold shower and maybe a hard right hook to his jaw. There had to be something to knock some sense into him.

It took more willpower than he thought he had to move her away from him. Bailey's smile faded, and even though her breathing was still way too fast, the heat from the kiss soon started to fade, and reality sank in.

"Oh," she said in the same tone a person might use if they'd walked in on their parents having sex.

"Yeah, *oh,*" Parker was about to apologize, to tell her he'd do his best to make sure that didn't happen again, but Bailey spoke first.

"You stopped kissing me because of your wife? You're still grieving for her?"

"What?" And it was a miracle he managed to say that. The questions really threw him because he damn sure hadn't been thinking of Amy when he'd kissed Bailey.

That caused a sudden surge of guilt.

"You're not ready to move on," Bailey continued. "I understand that." She shook her head and stepped away, walking to the window. "Except I really don't. I've never had someone that important in life. Someone that means everything to me."

Well, Amy had been that—his everything. Too bad Parker had never told her or shown her. That's because he'd always put the job first.

Just as he was doing now.

Parker scowled at that realization and assured himself that this was different. Bailey was in danger, and if he lost focus, that could get her killed. When he'd been on army assignments, Amy had been safe.

Or so he'd thought.

Bad weather and slick roads had been Amy's danger. Not exactly a stalker, but it had turned out to be just as lethal.

"Oh, God," he heard Bailey whisper.

At first, Parker thought this was just more of their conversation about why he'd stopped that kiss, but Bailey wasn't looking at him. She had her attention fastened to the window.

Parker raced across the room and looked out. Hell. It was the black car from the surveillance footage, but this time it wasn't moving. It was stopped in the side parking lot of the day care, and the window was down.

Parker could see the driver.

It wasn't Sidney Burrell, that's for sure. But this was a male in his early to mid-twenties, brown hair.

Parker drew his gun. "Call Sheriff Hale," he told Bailey. He also took out his phone and snapped a picture of the driver. "Send this to Corps headquarters and have them put the photo through the facial-recognition software." He shoved his phone into Bailey's hand and ran toward the door.

"Where are you going?" Bailey called out.

"I'm going after this SOB. Lock down the place once I'm outside, keep everyone away from the windows and doors and make those calls to the sheriff and Corps headquarters."

Bailey followed him down the stairs. "You should wait until the sheriff gets here."

Parker paused at the front door. "It might be too late then. If I catch this guy, then this all ends today." Hopefully. There was still the situation with Sidney, but Parker would deal with that later.

For now, he had a stalker to catch.

"Remember, lock the doors and stay inside," he warned Bailey.

Parker wished he could take the time to assure her that all would be well, but it was an assurance he couldn't back up, and besides there wasn't time. He didn't want that car driving away.

He hurried outside and was relieved when he heard Bailey calling the sheriff while she locked the door.

Parker raced down the porch steps and into the yard. The black car was on the left side of the building, but he went to the right so he could come up behind the vehicle. He had no idea if the driver was armed, but he had to assume he was. Parker also had to assume this guy didn't have anything good in mind. After all, he'd eluded the sheriff for the past twenty-four hours, and now he had shown up and was sitting there like an animal ready to attack.

But why?

Was this to intimidate Bailey?

If so, then this moron had certainly heard by now that Bailey had a bodyguard, and if not, he was about to find out the hard way.

With his gun ready, Parker ran to the back of the day care and cut through the playground. When he got to the corner of the building, he stopped and peered around it.

The black car was still there, and the engine was running.

It was parked facing Main Street, a good thing because that meant Parker stood a better chance of sneaking up on the man.

Both the driver's-side and passenger's windows were down, and it was hardly the weather for it. It was close to a hundred degrees, and the sun was bearing down on the concrete parking lot.

There didn't appear to be anyone else in the vehicle, just the driver. Parker glanced around to the other side of the parking lot. To the street. There was some light traffic, but there didn't seem to be anyone else waiting to jump out and assist this stalking driver.

Parker inched out from the building and behind a mountain laurel shrub. It didn't provide much cover, but it got him a few feet closer. Still, there were at least twenty yards between him and that car.

He took a deep breath, tightened his grip on his gun and went for it. He didn't run. Parker just took aim and began to walk toward the car.

As he got closer, he got a better look at the guy thanks to the angle of the passenger's-side mirror. The man had his attention nailed to the second-floor window where Bailey's office was located.

The anger slammed through Parker. This SOB was looking for her, probably hoping that she was sitting up there cowering in fear. But he knew Bailey. And she was no doubt making those calls and trying to figure out the identity of this jerk.

"Put your hands on the steering wheel so I can see them," Parker called out.

The man didn't move. He didn't put his hands on the steering wheel, either. He just slid his gaze from the window to the mirror so that he was looking at Parker.

Was this about to turn into an ambush?

Parker glanced around again but didn't see anyone.

"I said put your hands where I can see them." Parker walked closer, his gun pointed right at the driver.

He couldn't shoot him, of course, not this close to the day-care building, but Parker hoped the gun would be intimidating enough. Besides, he figured this guy was a coward. Most stalkers were.

As if he had all the time in the world and nothing to be concerned about, the man finally put his hands on the steering wheel. No gun. But he had something in his left hand.

It was a piece of paper.

"Who are you?" Parker demanded. He went closer, eating up the distance between them. If he made it all the way to the car, he intended to drag the guy out and check to make sure he wasn't armed. Then, the sheriff could take him in for questioning.

But Parker wanted some answers now.

"What do you want with Bailey?" Parker asked. He approached the back of the vehicle and started to the side.

The man waited until Parker was just a few yards away, and his hand moved. He tossed the paper out the window and then slammed on the accelerator.

"Stop!" Parker yelled, and he took aim, hoping it would cause the guy to stop.

It didn't.

The driver flew out of the parking lot and directly onto Main Street. Right into traffic. Two vehicles had to swerve to keep from hitting the car. There were the sounds of horns honking and brakes squealing. The sound of a police siren, too. But the driver maneuvered through the now stopped cars and sped away.

Parker ran after him.

Maybe the idiot would crash into something. Hopefully, not another car or person, but as crazy as he was driving, there was a good chance he would lose control of the vehicle.

From the corner of his eye, Parker saw the sheriff pull into the other side of the day-care parking lot and drive around to where moments earlier that black car had been parked. Parker motioned back toward the street where he was running. He didn't want to lose sight of that black car because the sheriff and he could then go in pursuit.

Parker's heart was racing by the time he made it to the sidewalk of Main Street, and his gaze whipped to the east, the direction the driver had taken.

Nothing.

The car was already out of sight.

Parker cursed, turned and raced back toward the sheriff who had parked and gotten out. "I've already radioed my deputy," Sheriff Hale told him. "He'll see if he can pick up the driver's trail."

Not much chance of that. The guy had already eluded them once, and Parker's frustration about that must have come through in every inch of his body language.

The sheriff stooped down to pick up the paper the driver had tossed out.

"Wait," Parker warned. "That might have prints we can use to ID the guy. He wasn't wearing gloves."

"We know who he is, Parker," the sheriff told him. He picked up the paper. "His name is Chester Herman."

Parker shook his head and looked up at the window. Bailey was there, staring down at him and obviously waiting for news. "How did you find out his identity?"

"Bailey called Corps headquarters right after she got

off the phone with me, and by the time I made it over here, they already had a match." Sheriff Hale unfolded the paper and looked at it.

Parker was thankful that Bailey's call had gotten such quick results, but he knew what this meant. "They were able to identify him so quickly because this Chester Herman has a police record."

The sheriff nodded. "He's a former militia troublemaker. He spent about a year behind bars on an illegal weapons' charge."

"That's the only jail time he's had?" Parker pressed. Bailey was motioning for him to come to her, but Parker first had to get some answers and a look at that paper.

"Yeah. That's not enough?"

Maybe. But something didn't fit. A stalker who would escalate to this level usually had a history of related crimes. Other stalkings, vandalism, maybe even assault.

The sheriff's phone rang, and he glanced at the screen. "It's Bailey."

Of course she would call the sheriff since Parker didn't have his phone. He'd given it to her after he took the photo of Chester Herman.

"Just how dangerous is this man?" Parker pressed the sheriff.

Sheriff Hale took a deep breath. "Read it for yourself." He mumbled some profanity and handed Parker the paper he'd picked up.

Chapter Seven

"Are you okay?" Parker asked her.

Bailey nodded, but that nod was a lie. She wasn't okay. She was in danger, and the note that Chester Herman had tossed from his car window was proof of that.

This isn't over. Hope you enjoy what I have planned for you.

The note wasn't just sick and disturbing, it infuriated her. This moron was dictating her life, and why? Maybe because he was just crazy, or maybe he had some kind of point he wanted to make about how he disapproved of her mother's strong stance against militia groups.

Either way, Bailey felt like a hostage.

It had taken her all afternoon and into the early evening to make the calls and do the paperwork, but she had officially closed Cradles to Crayons, put her staff on paid leave, and now, thanks to Chester Herman, she couldn't even go home. Parker had taken her there just long enough to pack a suitcase, and then they'd gone for a quick supper at the Talk of the Town.

Now they were driving to his place.

She wanted her own bed. Her own life. But she didn't put up a fight about going to Parker's house. She was exhausted even though it was only a little past nine. Her body or her mind couldn't handle much more of this kind of stress.

"Last chance," Parker reminded her. "I can take you out to your family ranch, and you can stay there."

Yes, she could do that, and then she would be trapped under the same roof with her micromanaging mother and Tim, who gave her the creeps. If she had to be trapped somewhere, she preferred it to be with Parker and his son.

But then that created a whole new set of issues to deal with.

Despite Parker's assurance that it would be all right, Zach might not want her there at his house. If Bailey picked up on any of those vibes, then she would have to head to the ranch.

Of course, Zach was not her worst concern.

Parker was.

And this attraction between them.

The kiss in her office had nearly gotten out of hand, and she couldn't risk that again. Well, she could.

But Parker couldn't.

He was obviously still nursing a broken heart from his wife's death, and giving in to the attraction might be satisfying physically, but Parker would soon resent himself and her. She didn't need that, and neither did Parker and Zach. So, she had to put up some emotional barriers.

Or at least try.

Parker turned onto his street, and thanks to plenty of overhead lights, she spotted the small ranch-style house. It was in an older neighborhood with lots of mature shade trees and blooming shrubs. The lawns weren't so manicured as on her street, but it had a welcome-home feel to it.

Especially with the basketball hoop in the driveway.

She smiled, recalling the conversation she'd had with Zach. Maybe she could talk him into shooting baskets with her. It might help to take the edge off this powder keg of energy and emotions inside her.

Parker used the remote control clipped to his visor to open the garage, and once he'd retrieved her suitcase from the back, they entered the house through a small pass-through laundry room.

"The guest room is this way," Parker stated, turning on lights as they walked.

Bailey followed him across the kitchen. It was sparse and a little outdated with its green tiles and white appliances. It was also spotless except for what was left of a take-out dinner from Talk of the Town and a half-empty glass of milk on the counter.

Other than the leftovers, there were no personal touches. No knickknacks, only a Dallas Mavericks magnet on the fridge.

Zach's doing, no doubt.

The cupboard above the fridge had a combination lock on it—causing her to wonder what Parker considered worthy of locking away.

From the kitchen she could see the living room at the

front of the house. Also sparse, but like the kitchen, it was neat and ordered. Nothing out of place. That probably had to do with Parker's military training. There hadn't been anything out of place in his truck, either. Not even a discarded gum wrapper or gas receipt.

"Zach's room," Parker said as they passed the first of four doors in the hall. There was a keep-out sign, and she heard the music blaring. "Turn down the volume and use your headphones!" Parker called out and gave one sharp rap on the wall. "Ms. Lockhart's here."

Earlier, she'd heard Parker phone his son to tell him that she would be staying with them a few days, but what Bailey hadn't heard was Zach's reaction.

Parker tipped his head to the door next to Zach's. "That's the bathroom. Normally, it's Zach's, but he'll use the one in my bedroom while you're here."

"I don't mind sharing," she commented. "I don't want to disrupt his routine."

"He doesn't mind," Parker said as gospel. Bailey made a mental note to discuss it with Zach because he might indeed *mind*.

"My room is the last one. It's at the front of the house." Parker threw open the only door that remained. The one next to his.

The guest room.

Definitely no frills. A double bed with a beige comforter, a bare dresser and nightstand. Blinds but no curtains. There was a single landscape picture on the off-white walls.

"It isn't much," Parker mumbled.

"Looks pretty good to me," she assured him. "When

you first said I'd be staying at your place, I had visions of sleeping on an army cot."

"The army cot's in the closet." Since he said it in the same tone as his previous sentence, it took her a moment to realize it was a joke.

He set her suitcase on the floor and looked at her. "How are you really doing?"

Bailey considered another lie, but what would be the point? Parker obviously knew that Chester's threatening note had shaken her.

"The sheriff is still looking for Chester," Parker reminded her. "There's an APB out on him. Plus, the people at Corps headquarters are checking into his background to see if they can figure out where to find him."

Bailey didn't doubt that the man would soon be found, but she was worried that the authorities wouldn't have anything to hold him. After all, the only new crime that he'd committed was littering, because he could explain away the note by saying someone had left it for him or that it was joke.

It didn't feel like a joke.

Her heavy sigh made Parker slip his arm around her and pull her closer.

Bailey automatically stiffened. "Remember what happened the last time you tried to comfort me."

The corner of his mouth lifted in that oh-so-sexy half smile of his, and he brushed a kiss on her forehead. "Zach's just up the hall," he reminded her.

Zach was a built-in chaperone, and one they apparently needed because the heat of his chaste kiss on her forehead reminded her of his other kiss. The kiss that had turned her from being interested in Parker to being *extremely* interested.

"I don't have the time or energy for sex," she said, then winced. Bailey blamed it on the fatigue because she hadn't expected to be so blunt.

Something went through his eyes. Eyes more blue than gray at the moment. Those eyes were like a mood ring, and the blue meant this was a good if not perhaps soon-to-be interesting moment.

He looked as if she'd just thrown down the gauntlet.

And he lowered his head, put his mouth to hers and kissed her. Nothing chaste this time. It was hot and clever and probably curled her toes. It certainly made her feel as if she were melting.

"There's always energy for sex. *Always,*" he joked, pulling back. He continued to stare at her. His expression continued to morph until she saw something else—frustration.

"Sorry," he mumbled.

She would have given him a lecture about playing with fire, if her body hadn't been one big flame. And if she hadn't heard Zach come into the hall.

She and Parker separated immediately. Parker stepped out of the guest room, and once Bailey had leveled her breathing, she did the same.

"Ms. Lockhart," Zach greeted, his attention zooming right past his dad to land on her. "I got my stuff out of the bathroom. Sometimes when you flush the toilet, you have to jiggle the handle to make it stop running." And he blushed a little as if he regretted bringing it up.

"Thanks. I'll remember that."

Parker's cell phone rang, and he glanced down at the screen. "It's Corps headquarters." He glanced at Zach. "Why don't you take Bailey to the kitchen and show her around? Clean up your dinner mess, too." He checked his watch despite the fact his phone continued to ring. "Lights out for you in one hour," he told Zach.

"Yes, sir." Zach looked even more embarrassed.

"I don't know if I can last an hour," Bailey mumbled to the boy, and she watched as Parker went into his room, no doubt to deal with that call. He even shut the door.

She wondered why he hadn't answered it in front of her. Probably because he didn't want to upset her with potentially more bad news. Of course, that only upset her more. Yes, she was exhausted, but she didn't want Parker or anyone else sheltering her.

Even if he was already doing that—literally—by having her at his house.

Bailey sighed. Parker was certainly creating a lot of conflict inside her, and that was a dangerous mix with the fire from the attraction.

"Don't worry. My dad won't give you any rules," Zach said, leading her into the kitchen. He cleaned up the remains of his dinner, putting the bag in the trash and the glass in the dishwasher.

"You eat at the Talk of the Town a lot?" she asked.

"Yeah. Dad's not much of a cook so he told the lady at the café to just send him a bill at the end of each week.

But there's plenty in the freezer." He opened it for her to see the precisely stacked rows of microwave dinners and snacks. "Plenty of fruit and junk, too. One of his rules is I gotta eat the healthy junk at least three times a day."

The fridge was indeed stocked, and a crazy thought flashed through her head. Did Parker make love with the same precision he ran the rest of his life?

That caused the fire to flame up inside her again.

And she cursed herself. She really had to find a way around this heated obsession with Parker.

"There's guns up there," Zach said, pointing to the cupboard with the combination lock. "They're for dad's job. Don't know why he has to keep them locked. It's not like I'd touch them or anything. I'm not a kid anymore."

No. But Bailey understood the safety precaution and was glad Parker had taken it.

"Want me to fix you anything?" Zach asked. "Like a snack, I mean? I can do nachos or something."

"No, thanks. But I wouldn't say no to a glass of milk."

Zach smiled a little, and she thought he might be pleased at being able to do something for her. He poured himself a glass as well and leaned against the counter. Bailey sat on one of the bar stools.

"So, how was basketball camp?" she asked.

"Okay, I guess. I mean, I'm pretty sure I can start for the team next season, but I still gotta work on that three-point shot." He looked everywhere but at her. "Guess you don't come to the games, huh? I'm not sure how often my dad can come. He stays busy with work. A lot," Zach added.

"I haven't been to any of the games, not in a while. But I could go this season and watch you play." She tried to gauge his expression. "If that's all right. I wouldn't want to…impose or anything. I remember when I was your age. *Barely.* But I wavered between being embarrassed by my mother and her friends to being semi-thankful that she could make it to any of my games. She had a very busy schedule, too."

"I wouldn't be embarrassed if you came," he quickly assured her. "Your dad didn't come and watch you play?"

"He died when I was about your age." Cancer. It had struck hard and fast and had left Bailey with a pain she still felt today. It had also left her mother a young widow with three children to raise on her own.

"Yeah." Zach downed half the glass of milk like a man taking a shot of whiskey. "Like my mom."

"Like your mom," Bailey repeated, and she could practically feel his pain.

She resisted going to him and putting her arms around him, but that's what she wanted to do. He was all arms and legs, lanky and tall, but he also had a little-boy-lost look about him. It wasn't just basketball that Zach and she had in common. Losing a parent was a powerful bond.

"You were close to your mother?" Bailey asked.

Zach nodded. "She was going to have a baby when she died. My sister. I woulda liked having a little sister."

Oh, mercy. Bailey had to blink back the tears. "Your

dad took their deaths hard, too," she said because she didn't know what else to say.

"He did," Zach agreed. And that surprised her. Thirteen wasn't a big age for empathy. "He's still taking it really hard. That's why I'm glad you're here. Not that you two are like dating or anything. I know he's your bodyguard, but I think he kinda likes you."

Bailey blinked, totally surprised and totally not knowing how to respond. "I think I kind of like him, too." Sheesh. She shouldn't be confessing this to Parker's son.

But Zach smiled that half smile that made him look so much like his dad. "He'll keep you safe, you know. Because that's what he does. He's like a superhero soldier. I saw him once working out in a pretend fight at the army base. He's real strong and fast. I don't think a bad guy stands a chance with him around."

"Good." And Bailey believed that. Parker would do anything and everything to protect her.

Zach finished his milk, rinsed his glass and put it in the dishwasher. He kept his back to her, but she didn't need to see his face to know that his mood had changed. "It's scary though. Because there's always something that can stop a superhero. I don't think my dad could live if he got shot. I think that would kill him like the car wreck killed my mom and sister. And then, I'd be, like, an orphan."

She heard his voice crack, saw his shoulders slump, and nothing could have stopped her from setting her own glass aside and going to him. Bailey caught onto his arm and turned him toward her.

"We got no other family," Zach added. "That's why Dad had to give up his army job when mom died. He had to give it up to take care of me." His voice broke again. "My dad's all I got. Without him, I'd have no place to go."

"Nothing is going to happen to your dad," she consoled.

"It could. Bad things happen all the time, and he's always out there with the bad guys."

Bailey put her arms around him. "Your dad is smart, and he knows how important it is to stay safe. Because of you. Because he loves you."

Zach looked at her as if she'd sprouted a third eye. "He told you that?"

"He didn't have to. I know he loves you." Zach tried to shrug, but Bailey held on and forced eye contact. "Your father loves you."

His surprise was genuine. He honestly hadn't known that he was the center of Parker's life.

Zach eased back, but she kept her hand on his arm. "Something could still happen. I could still be an orphan, and they'd sent me to one of those places with other orphans. They're like places where kids have to go when no one else wants them."

"That's not going to happen," Bailey reassured him.

"But it could," Zach argued.

Bailey stooped down so they were at eye level. "No, because I wouldn't let them send you to a place like that. I would adopt you myself."

She meant it. She barely knew this boy, but she

wouldn't let him just be sucked up into foster care. Still, that was something she shouldn't have been so adamant about.

Zach's gaze widened, and she whipped around to see Parker standing in the doorway. He'd obviously heard all or most of what she'd said.

The silence was suddenly thick and uncomfortable.

Parker volleyed glances between Zach and her, and Bailey stepped away, shoving her hands into her pockets. "Uh, Zach and I were just talking."

Parker didn't respond to that except for the one uneven breath that he took.

"G'night," Zach mumbled, and he shot past them and out of the kitchen.

Bailey was about to explain that entire conversation, but Parker spoke before she could say anything. "Nothing on Chester Herman," he offered first, "but I did get some interesting information on Penske."

With everything else going on, she'd forgotten, he'd had Corps Security and Investigations do a background check on her mother's bodyguard. "Please don't tell me that Tim has a sealed juvenile record or was involved in a militia group?"

Parker shook his head. "But he does have a weird obsession with you. Did you know he's told some of his friends that you two are dating?"

"What?" Bailey hadn't thought the night could bring any more surprises, but she'd obviously been wrong.

"He told one friend that he plans to take you on a cruise. And when the Corps investigator dug into his financials, he learned that last week Tim ordered a white gold ring with diamonds and a ruby heart from a jeweler in Amarillo. He's having your name, and his, engraved on the inside band."

Oh, sheesh. How creepy was that? "I haven't done anything to make him believe I'm interested in him."

"Well, he's interested in you."

Obviously. Bailey huffed and checked the time. Her mother was probably getting ready for bed. "I'll call Mom first thing in the morning," Bailey insisted.

"I'd rather you not mention that it was Corps Security and Investigations that had Tim checked," Parker explained. "It might cause some tension between Bart and your mother."

Bailey nodded. She didn't want that. Bart was the one friend her mother could turn to right now, and Bailey didn't want her to lose that. "I'll be delicate. I'll just say I've heard rumors and go from there."

She paused, hesitated, but Parker didn't say anything else. Was he angry at what she'd said to Zach? If so, she was too tired to argue with him. "I think I'll turn in early. It's been a long day."

"Yeah." But then Parker stepped in front of her when she moved. "You told my son that you'd adopt him if something happened to me?"

Bailey winced. "Uh, I did say that. I just sort of blurted it out because he was upset over the idea of losing you. I couldn't stand to see him in pain like that. I'm sorry. I shouldn't—"

"Don't make him promises you can't keep," Parker warned.

That improved her posture. Bailey pulled back her

shoulders and stared at him. "Who says I won't keep it? It might have been a spur-of-the-moment comment, but it wasn't lip service. If something happened to you…" that required a deep breath "…I wouldn't let the state put Zach in foster care."

"You'd adopt him?" Parker clarified. Those eyes were dark gray now.

"Yes." And she didn't hesitate. "What? You don't think I'd be a good mother?"

"You'd be an excellent one." He mumbled some profanity and shook his head. "I just don't want you to feel obligated to Zach because you and I have the hots for each other."

Bailey aimed her index finger at him. "What I feel for you has nothing to do with your son. Okay, maybe it does a little. I mean, I wouldn't have met him if it weren't for you, but now that I know him, I just wouldn't turn my back if something went wrong. That's not the kind of person I am. And besides, Zach's a good kid. I'd be the one getting the good deal if I got to raise him."

Parker just stared at her, and she saw all those unspoken things in his eyes. Old wounds, old hurt, that were still fresh and raw. "He is a good kid," he whispered. "Too bad he doesn't have a father he can love."

"What?" Bailey gave him the look Zach had given her earlier. The third-eye-sprouted look. "He loves you. He's very proud of you."

Parker shook his head, mumbled no and shook his head again.

Bailey nodded, mumbled yes and nodded again. "He's thinks you're a superhero GI, and the thing he fears most is losing you. That's why the adoption discussion even came up. He can't bear the thought of losing his dad."

Parker's mouth dropped open, and he looked ready to argue with her about that. But he didn't. He swallowed hard and motioned toward Zach's door. "I should, um, try to talk to him or something."

"Yes, you should." Bailey lifted her hands. "Look, I don't believe for a minute that one heart-to-heart talk will end a teenage boy's surliness. Some of that's inevitable. I have a brother eleven years younger than I am, and I was on the receiving end of a lot of that surliness. But I think it'll help for Zach to hear that you love him and that you'll do everything to make sure you stay safe for him."

Still obviously in deep thought, Parker ran his hand down the length of her arm. "Thanks." And he brushed another chaste kisses on her forehead.

Parker turned to leave. Then, stopped. He eased back around to face her.

His hand whipped behind her neck, and he snapped her to him for a kiss of a different kind. His mouth moved over hers, giving and taking at the same time, until the taste of him was in her mouth. Until she was boneless and breathless.

Until she wanted him more than she'd ever wanted anything.

"Come to my bed tonight," Parker drawled against her mouth. And with that searing invitation, he let go of her and walked away toward Zach's room.

Oh, mercy.

She was in trouble here.

Bailey started to call out to him, to give him a chance to rethink that offer that could complicate beyond belief an already complicated situation. It could also give them one of the best nights ever.

Her body was tingling just thinking about it. All that precision. All that superhero strength. All those muscles. She wasn't a shallow woman, but the thought of getting her hands on his body made her mouth water, literally.

Cursing under her breath, she slapped off the lights in case Parker returned. She didn't want him to see her practically drooling, especially since she should be doing something, anything, to talk herself of what she really wanted to do.

Bailey *really* wanted to go to his bed tonight.

She went to the fridge and took out one of the long-neck bottles of beer. Beer wasn't her favorite, but she hoped it would settle her nerves. Bailey opened the bottle and went to the sink to look under the counter for the garbage so she could discard the cap.

Something in the backyard caught her eye. Some kind of movement. Maybe.

Bailey leaned closer to the glass, trying to pick through the unfamiliar surroundings and sounds. The lawn, the shrubs, the trees. The nighttime summer breeze was playing with a wind chime on one of the lower branches of a sprawling live oak. The cicadas were making themselves heard, too.

She was about to turn away, to head off to bed and

give Parker's invitation more thought, but she saw the movement again near the tree with the wind chime.

This part of Texas was filled with squirrels, raccoons, owls and too many birds to name. It could be any one of those creatures. Maybe even a coyote because they sometimes wandered into residential areas. Also, there was a hunter's moon, and that always created some spooky shadows. She reminded herself that it was probably nothing more than her overly stressed imagination.

But Bailey saw it then. It wasn't an animal. Nor a shadow.

It was a man.

Chapter Eight

It took Parker several minutes to work up enough nerve to knock on Zach's door. He'd faced enemy fire without flinching, but the thought of having a heart-to-heart with his son terrified him.

Bailey sure didn't have that same problem.

She was a natural with Zach, and Parker might have been envious of her ease of conversation with his teenage son if he hadn't been just so damn thankful that Zach had someone that he could communicate with.

"Yeah?" Zach answered when Parker knocked.

"It's me. May I come in?"

Silence for several *long* moments. "I guess. What's wrong?"

"Nothing's wrong." Parker opened the door and saw Zach stretched out on the bed reading a comic book.

"It's not time for lights-out yet," Zach grumbled.

"No. It's not." Though he had noticed when Bailey turned off the kitchen light. She was likely exhausted and ready to bed. Probably too exhausted to take him up on his offer—an offer Parker could kick himself for now. Talk about getting caught up in the heat of the moment.

But for now, this moment belonged to his son.

Parker took a deep breath and bracketed his hands on the door frame. "I heard some of what Bailey said to you and wondered if you wanted to talk about it."

There. The ball was now in his son's court.

Zach shrugged and kept his eyes nailed to the comic book. "I was just worried about some things. That's all."

Yes. Worried that Parker was going to be killed and that Zach would become an orphan. He hated that his son had even considered something like that, but when Parker had been in the army, that had always been a possibility. Too bad he'd never thought to discuss it with Zach.

Zach opened his mouth to say something, but the sound stopped him. It was Bailey. Not exactly a scream, but it was close.

"Parker! There's a man in the backyard."

"Stay here," Parker told his son. He hit the light switch to turn it off and drew his gun. Zach's blinds were open, and he considered having his son close them, but he didn't want Zach near the window.

"Bailey, get down!" Parker called out to her.

Parker was only a few steps away from the kitchen, and even though the lights were already off, he spotted her immediately. She was crouched down by the sink.

"I saw a man standing behind the tree with the wind chime," she detailed. Her voice was a tangle of nerves and adrenaline.

"Crawl away from the window," Parker instructed.

If this guy tried to break in, he'd probably use either the window or the back door, both of which had panes, and Parker didn't want to risk Bailey being hit with broken glass.

Parker considered calling 9-1-1. Sheriff Hale or one of his deputies could be out in less than ten minutes, but he wanted to know what they were up against first.

He could see part of the yard from where he was standing but not the tree in question. Parker waited until Bailey had moved against the snack bar before he approached the window. He kept his gun ready but prayed he didn't have to use it.

Parker had only lived in this particular house a few weeks, and he didn't know all of his neighbors' habits. Maybe this was just someone out for a nighttime stroll or a smoke. However, Parker had to be ready for the worst.

Chester Herman's note slammed through Parker's head. *This isn't over. Hope you enjoy what I have planned for you.*

Had Chester planned a visit to scare Bailey? Well, if so, it was working. He could tell from her heavy breathing that she was scared.

Parker inched closer, his attention nailed to the backyard. He saw the tree, the wind chimes, but he couldn't see a man.

"He's not there," Parker mumbled.

"I saw someone," Bailey pled. "I swear, I did."

"I believe you. He might be behind the tree now." Or he could have moved, perhaps even closer to the house.

There were a lot of shrubs where a person could hide. He made a mental note to cut them down.

Parker moved to the other side of the window, so that he'd have a different angle. Still no sign of this mystery man. So, he reached over and turned on the back-porch lights. They were bright, positioned on both ends of the porch, and they illuminated most of the grounds, including the area by the tree.

At first, the extra light didn't help, but Parker waited and finally saw something move. Not by the tree itself but just beyond it where there was a greenbelt of thick shrubs and foliage that separated the houses on his street from a dry creek bed.

Yeah. It was definitely a man.

"I see him," Parker relayed to Bailey, causing her to gasp. "He's dressed head to toe in black." Not exactly the attire of someone out for a neighborly walk.

Parker reached for his phone to call the sheriff, but the man in black moved. He evaporated into the shadows. For a moment, Parker thought the guy would just leave and this would end. Well, end for Bailey. It would mean Parker would keep watch all night. But then the saw it.

The glint of metal.

It was just a little flash, but it was a huge warning for Parker. "Get flat down on the floor!" he shouted to Bailey, and he jumped to the side.

The shot slammed into the back of the house.

It hit one of the limestone posts that supported the porch roof. But something was off with the sound. That wasn't the sound a normal bullet would make, but Parker had seen the flash associated with the shot.

The gunman was using a silencer.

"Dad?" Zach called out.

Oh, hell. He hadn't forgotten for one second that his son was in the house, but the terror in Zach's voice cut Parker to the core. How dare this SOB threaten Bailey and his son this way.

"Get under your bed," Parker told Zach. "And don't come out until I tell you it's safe." He tried to keep his voice level and calm, and while he kept watch out the window he called 9-1-1 and requested assistance.

Parker didn't know what kind of firepower their attacker had so while he eyed the door, he unlocked the cupboard so he could take out a SIG SAUER. It was a more powerful weapon than the gun he carried in his ankle holster, and he might need greater firepower before this was over.

"I'll go to Zach," Bailey insisted, and she started crawling across the floor to the hall.

"Don't get near the windows," Parker warned. "You know how to shoot?"

Bailey gave a shaky nod. "My dad taught me."

Parker handed her the smaller gun. Her fingers were trembling, and Parker hoped like hell that she didn't have to use it.

She crawled away, and Parker heard when she knocked on Zach's door. He didn't look in their direction, but he listened as his son let Bailey into the room. Maybe they could keep each other calm while he took care of this latest situation.

He waited, his attention on the shadows where he'd last seen the gunman. There was another glint of metal, and Parker braced himself.

The second shot smacked into the same limestone porch post. It had the same sound as the first. More of a swish than a blast.

The stone porch was a blessing; the house's best defense. It wouldn't be long before the sheriff arrived. Parker didn't know if Sheriff Hale would make a silent approach without the use of his sirens, but it didn't matter. The gunman could no doubt see the street, and he would notice an approaching cruiser.

And then he'd try to run away.

Parker didn't want to let that happen.

The moment the sheriff or his deputy arrived, Parker intended to go after this SOB. It was the only way to stop the threats against Bailey and now his son.

A third shot slammed into the porch post. Nowhere near the glass or the door. Nowhere near Parker or Zach's bedrooms.

Hell.

It hit Parker then. Chester Herman was a former militia member and no doubt had tons of experience with firearms. He wouldn't have missed the most vulnerable points of entry. No. If he'd wanted to get to Bailey, then the attack would have started on the side of the house where the bedrooms were located.

This was a diversion.

"Someone's trying to break in!" Bailey yelled.

Parker's heart went to his knees, and he raced out of the kitchen and into the hall. Zach's door was locked so he kicked it down. He already had his left hand bracketing his wrist, and his gun was ready. The moment the door was out of his way, he took aim.

He couldn't fire unless the gunman actually came through the window because he couldn't risk shooting one of his neighbors or having the bullet ricochet and hit Bailey or Zach.

Parker got just a glimpse of the man dressed in black before he darted away. It appeared to be the same man he'd seen earlier. The man who'd just fired shots at the porch posts.

How could this guy be in two places at once?

Maybe this was an accomplice? Chester had been alone in the car earlier, but that didn't mean he hadn't brought someone along to terrorize Bailey. Besides, Parker wasn't even sure this was Chester. He hadn't been able to make out the guy's face in the darkness.

Outside, he heard the police siren, but Parker kept his attention focused on his son's bedroom window and the other possible entry points in the house. The gunman might make a last-ditch effort to break in and start shooting before the cruiser arrived at the house.

Bailey and Zach were on the floor, and she had her body covering his. Protecting him. She had a death grip on the gun Parker had given her, and while she looked terrified, she also looked determined. She wasn't going to let this goon get anywhere near Zach.

The blue swirls of lights from the cruiser slashed through the house, and Parker's phone rang. He answered it but kept watch.

"Where is he?" Sheriff Hale asked.

"The west side of the house. He's armed, has fired shots, and he just tried to break in through the window."

"Stay inside with Bailey and your boy," the sheriff told him. "We'll take care of this."

Parker's first instinct was to be out there in the middle of the fight, but his son and Bailey were the only things that were important now. He had to stay with them, to protect them if the gunman made it into the house, because maybe this was just another phase of the diversion.

The seconds crawled by, each of them marked with a heavy thud of Parker's heartbeat. Neither Bailey nor Zach said a thing, but he could hear them breathing. He could also taste their fear, and Parker hated that he hadn't been able to stop this from happening. This was a nightmare that Zach would remember for the rest of his life, and his already had too many nightmares as it was.

"Told you Dad was like a superhero," Parker heard Zach whisper to Bailey.

"Yes, you did," she whispered back.

Parker tried to shut them out, tried not to hear what might have been pride in his son's voice. He would remember those words for the rest of his life, but for now Parker pushed them aside.

And waited.

Parker's phone rang again, the sounds shooting through the nearly silent room, and when he saw the caller was Sheriff Hale, he answered it immediately.

"Did you find him?" Parker asked the sheriff.

"No." The sheriff cursed, and it wasn't mild profanity, either. "But we found something else. You need to get out here and see this."

Chapter Nine

Bailey couldn't get the images out of her head. The man dressed all in black hiding next to the tree. The bullets he'd fired into Parker's house.

The gun he had left in the yard.

Even now with her eyes closed, Bailey could see it. Parker had called it an assault weapon rigged with a silencer, and it had been mounted on a pedestal, aimed right at the house. And according to Parker, the gunman had used a remote control to fire it. Three times.

Straight into Parker's house.

Sheriff Hale and Parker had agreed that the gun hadn't been aimed in such a way for the bullets to hit anyone inside. Just to scare them and allow time for someone like Chester Herman to break in and scare them some more.

Or rather scare *her*.

It had worked. She was scared, not just for herself but for Parker and especially Zach. Just because the bullets hadn't been aimed to kill them, it didn't mean the gunman couldn't have adjusted the gun to fire into another part of the house where Parker, Zach and she were.

Plus, the man had then tried to break into Zach's room. Did that mean he knew she was there?

Maybe.

The blinds were open. He could have seen her when she ran inside Zach's room. Bailey had done that to try to protect the boy, but she'd ended up putting him in immediate danger just by getting near him.

Knowing that she wouldn't fall back asleep, Bailey opened her eyes and glanced around the unfamiliar room. It was morning, already past eight, and she wasn't just in Parker's room, she was in his bed. She gave a hollow smile at the invitation he'd issued the night before.

Come to my bed tonight.

Well, she had ended up doing that, all right, after midnight when the sheriff and his deputies were certain that Chester Herman or whomever it was that had set up that gun was long gone.

But Parker hadn't been in his bed when she'd climbed into it, so exhausted that she hadn't even bothered to change her clothes.

Parker had eventually joined her in his bedroom after locking down everything in the house that he could lock and after arming the security system. Only then had Bailey managed to get some sleep.

She looked at Parker now. He was napping on a padded weight bench that looked absurdly small beneath his body.

Zach was on the floor asleep on an air mattress. Next

to the bed were a treadmill and a set of weights that went with the bench. The exercise equipment explained how Parker managed to keep all those muscles toned and in perfect shape.

Her gaze went to Parker again, and she wasn't surprised to see him staring at her. Heck, it was possible he hadn't even slept at all, that the closed eyes she'd seen earlier was a ruse to make her think he was getting some rest.

Bailey eased off the bed, grabbed her phone from the nightstand and motioned for him to go into the hall. They really needed to talk before Zach woke up.

On the way to the kitchen, she glanced in the open door of the bathroom and saw herself in the mirror. She groaned. No, it wasn't a time for vanity, but she looked a wreck.

Bailey followed Parker into the kitchen where he immediately started a pot of coffee. "Hungry?" he asked. He didn't wait for her answer. "You should eat something anyway."

He was right. She had no appetite, but with the search for Chester Herman still going on, this could turn out to be a long day. And another long night. Bailey grabbed a banana and the milk from the fridge. Parker handed her a glass that he took from the cupboard, and she sat on one of the bar stools at the counter.

"I guess there's no good news on the search for Chester?" she asked.

Parker shook his head and grabbed the bread, a jar of peanut butter, a knife and a saucer. "When I was at your house, I noticed that's what you had for breakfast."

It was her favorite. "You're observant."

"Not observant enough." Parker huffed and finished making the coffee as if he'd declared war on it. "I thought I was careful enough by making sure no one followed us here last night, but that gunman figured out you were here."

Yes. He had.

"But he could have learned that without following us. People talk in this town, and I'm sure everyone with email or a phone knows that I've closed Cradles to Crayons. They also know you're my bodyguard. It isn't much of a stretch to guess that if I'm not at home, I'd be here or the ranch."

So, did that mean this idiot had gone to her house, as well?

If so, hopefully he hadn't vandalized it or disturbed her neighbors. But she rethought that. If he had gone to either place, she would have already heard about it by now. People in Freedom didn't keep things to themselves.

Bailey forced herself to eat some of the peanut butter and bread, but it tasted like dust. Anything would at this point. Plus, there was a hard knot in her stomach that just wouldn't go away.

"What are we going to do, Parker?" And she was almost afraid to hear the answer.

"I made some calls last night." He paused long enough to pour them cups of the freshly made coffee. "Zach is going to stay with his friend Josh Bracken. Josh's dad is a deputy, and Bart is sending someone from Corps to keep an eye on the place. Zach will be safe."

"Yes," Bailey mumbled. "He'll be safe because he's not around me." The timing sucked. Parker and Zach would be apart just when they were starting to make some headway in their relationship.

"None of this is your fault."

She shrugged. "That doesn't change things. You should distance yourself, too."

"Right," he said in a harsh *no-way* tone. "I'm your bodyguard, Bailey. It's my job to protect you, and I never walk away from the job. Never."

"I'm just a job, huh?" That stung far more than she thought it would.

He scowled. "That's not what I meant. You're the job and you're Bailey—and don't ask me what the hell that means because I don't know. I don't know where these kissing and bed invitations are headed, but I do know I'm not going anywhere." He paused. "But maybe you should. I thought about having us go to the ranch to stay with your mother."

Bailey was shaking her head before he even finished. "Right." She mimicked his *no-way* tone. "I'd just bring the danger to my mother's doorstep. Plus, Tim is there. Remember, he ordered a ring with my name engraved inside? I sure don't trust him."

Parker gulped down some of the coffee. "I called about that, too. I spoke to Tim last night."

That brought her off the seat. "You called him?"

"I decided the direct approach was the best. He wasn't happy that I was asking the questions, but he did provide the answers. He denied telling any friends that you two were dating. And as for the ring, he said he ordered it as a gift for your mother. Her birthday's coming up, and the ring was supposed to be engraved with all her kids' names. Tim claims the jeweler just screwed up the order, that's all."

Bailey gave that some thought and sank back down onto the bar stool. That knot in her stomach was worse now. "Well, that's a tidy explanation. You believe him?"

Parker shook his head. "I don't know, but I do know that right now we have someone out there who's potentially a lot more dangerous."

"Chester Herman," she provided.

"And Sidney Burrell," Parker added. "I got an email report last night. Chester and Sidney went to the same high school, and from all accounts, they knew each other well."

Bailey didn't like the connection. "You think they're working together? Chester has the cause—he was furious with my mother's hard-nosed policies against militia groups—but maybe he hired Sidney to help him?"

"Could be. But we have no proof that Chester's actually done anything wrong. It might not have been him who fired those shots."

True, but after the threatening note he'd thrown into the parking lot of the day care, he was their number one suspect. But was Chester being set up by Sidney or someone else with a different motive?

Parker checked his watch, and with his coffee mug still in his hand, he headed for the hall. "I need to wake Zach. Josh's father will be here soon to pick him up."

"And I need to take a shower," she noted. She grabbed

her phone from the counter and followed him, not to his bedroom, but the guest room.

Bailey collected her things from her suitcase and went into the hall bathroom. She put her hair in a ponytail so it wouldn't get wet and took a short shower. Afterward, she dressed in a calf-length crinkled white skirt and a pink sleeveless top. Despite her less-than-ideal situation, she took the time to put on some makeup.

Even though she'd hurried, by the time Bailey made it out of the bathroom, Zach had packed and was on his way to the front door.

"Josh's father is here already?" Bailey asked, following Parker and Zach. Parker disarmed the security system and opened the door.

Zach nodded. "There's another basketball camp today, and his dad is taking us." He glanced at both of them and then at the car waiting for him in the driveway. "You'll, like, be okay, right?"

"Absolutely," Bailey said at the exact moment Parker answered, "Of course."

Parker put his hand on Zach's arm. "We'll catch this guy, and you'll be able to come home soon. I promise."

Zach stared at his dad as if he had something else to say, but he finally shook his head and looped the strap of his gym bag over his shoulder. He walked out. Parker and she stood there and watched until Deputy Bracken's car, and Zach, were out of sight.

Mercy. Zach wasn't even her son, and it hurt to see him leave. She couldn't imagine what Parker was feeling.

Parker closed the door, locked it and reengaged the security system by using the keypad mounted on the wall. He hitched his thumb toward the hall. "I need to shower and then I have to make a few calls, but I don't want you out of my sight for that long."

Okay. Bailey thought through her options. Was he asking her to shower with him? Her expression must have given away what she was thinking because Parker sighed and shook his head.

"I also can't have that kind of distraction," he added with regret in his voice. He brushed a kiss on her forehead but immediately moved away from her and started for the bathroom. "I'll leave the door open," Parker stated as she followed him to his bedroom.

He stripped off his T-shirt and sent it sailing into a laundry basket just inside the adjoining bathroom, threw back the shower curtain and turned on the water full blast. "Stay close so I can hear and see you."

Bailey managed a nod. Didn't even attempt speech, not after getting a look at him shirtless. Oh, mercy. She'd been right about his body. It was perfect.

Well, except for the scars.

There were three of them—one on his left biceps, another on his right shoulder and a final one at the top of his left hip. She got a good look at that one when he unzipped his jeans and started to lower them.

With his thumbs hooked on the waist of his jeans, Parker snagged her gaze. "If you're waiting for me to get modest, it's not going to happen, so you can close your eyes if you like."

Bailey tried to do that. She really tried, but she

couldn't make them close. It was like watching a Chippendale perform. Parker wasn't dancing or moving suggestively. He was just stripping down to his navy blue boxers which fit him like a glove.

The heat from the shower and her body washed over her, and Bailey finally closed her eyes just a split second before Parker removed his boxers.

She stood there, waiting, and imagining all sorts of things. She'd never been in the shower with a man, but the idea of being in there with Parker was very tempting.

What was wrong with her?

She wasn't the type to go head over heels like this. Yes, she enjoyed a man's company, but there had been a pitiful few that she'd trusted enough to take to her bed. But with Parker, those reservations didn't seem to exist.

Ironic, since the stakes with him were sky-high.

He was her bodyguard and as he'd said, he didn't need to be distracted. There was also Zach to consider. Starting an affair with a single dad who still had feelings for his late wife could be a nightmare. And when the relationship ended badly, and it would—all her relationships ended badly—then it wasn't just her who might get hurt. Zach might, as well.

Bailey had forgotten she was holding her phone until it rang. She nearly jumped out of her skin, and the sound caused Parker to pull back the shower curtain far enough for him to see her.

And for her to see him.

Bailey got a good look at his washboard abs with

that peek. She would have seen more if the slick shower curtain hadn't slipped forward.

"It's my sister, Chloe," Bailey commented. "Chloe," she repeated when she got it through her steam-induced thoughts that her sister rarely called her. And Bailey quickly put her on speakerphone. "Is something wrong?"

The alarmed question sent Parker scrambling out of the shower. No peek that time. Bailey got a full frontal view, and if it hadn't been for the possible importance of this call, she would have melted into a puddle.

"Yes, something's wrong," Chloe declared. "I have this fascist following me around."

Parker wound a towel around his waist and walked closer. "Have you called the sheriff?" Parker asked.

"Uh, no. Who is this?" Chloe demanded in a way that only Bailey's tattooed, extremely liberal kid sister could have demanded.

"Parker McKenna," Bailey provided. "He works for Corps Security and Investigations, and he's my bodyguard."

Chloe made a sound of exaggerated outrage. "Well, that explains that. Sis, did you think maybe you should tell me before you hired a CSI fascist to follow me around."

"I didn't." But Bailey certainly wished she had.

"I did," Parker volunteered. "The *fascist* is Harlan McClain, and he's one of the best. If your sister's stalker decides to turn his attention to other members of her family, Harlan will stop him."

Bailey drew in a breath of relief. Her sister wasn't in

danger, and Parker had taken steps to make sure things stayed that way. Bailey only wished she had thought of it.

"And I don't have a say in this?" Chloe howled.

"No!" Parker and Bailey said in unison.

"Parker did you, and me, a favor by sending Harlan McClain out to protect you," Bailey continued. "Chloe, things got ugly last night. Some idiot fired shots into Parker's house."

Chloe got quiet for a moment. "I heard, but I thought it was a rumor. You okay, sis?"

"I'm fine. But I don't want you taking any chances. Either go to the ranch with mom—"

"No way," Chloe interrupted. "I'd have to listen to her rant about my purple hair. And the new tat. Don't know if you've noticed, but Mom and I aren't on the same page when it comes to self-expression."

Translation: Chloe and their mother argued, and since both of them were bullheaded, they argued nonstop. "Then your only other option is to let Harlan McClain do his job. Understand?" Bailey asked.

"Yes." Chloe huffed. "I understand I'm stuck with a smart-mouth fascist who thinks my rebel personality is a pain in the butt."

"At times, like now, it is a pain," Bailey reminded her. "But you won't ditch him, and you'll do as he says. Promise me, Chloe."

More silence. "I promise," Chloe finally snarled. "So, is your bodyguard as much of a challenge as mine?"

Bailey looked at Parker. At the water sliding

down his chest. At his wet hair. At his perfect naked body—clothed only in a towel.

"Oh, he's a challenge, all right," Bailey mumbled. But not in the way her sister meant. "Bye, Chloe."

Bailey clicked End Call and tried to clear her head. No chance of that with Parker so close. "Thank you for sending someone out to protect her."

He lifted his shoulder. "It's just a precaution. This stalker is focused only on you. For now."

Yes, and while that was indeed sinister, her body wasn't feeling fear at the moment. It was desire, pure and simple.

Bailey suddenly didn't know what to do with her hands. Or her phone.

Or the rest of her.

She should probably turn and walk away because if she stayed, Bailey knew exactly what would happen.

Parker and she would have sex.

As much as she wanted that, and she *really* wanted that, she knew this would end badly.

"You worked things out in your head yet?" Parker asked, his voice all husky and low.

"Yes." But she wasn't sure exactly what she'd worked out. And Bailey didn't budge.

Parker did though.

He let go of the towel he wore, and it dropped to the floor. "Good," he drawled. "Because if we're going to screw this up, we might as well make it fast."

Parker slid his hand around the back of her neck and hauled her to him.

Chapter Ten

Parker knew exactly what he was doing. He also knew what he was doing was probably stupid. He should be distancing himself from Bailey. Emotionally, anyway.

But this was the opposite of distancing.

He kissed Bailey. Too hard. Too rough. And he pulled her ponytail holder and worked his fingers into her soft fragrant hair so that he controlled the movement of her head. Parker angled her so he could deepen the kiss.

That taste.

It was already familiar to him, but it felt just as new and powerful as the first time he'd kissed her. A dangerous mix of sex and heat. He was already a goner, and he'd barely touched her.

The fire of the kiss was making him crazy. So were her hands that she was sliding over his back. She was exploring, and judging from the sounds she was making, Bailey wanted him as much as he wanted her. Good. This couldn't be one-sided. If they were going to screw things up, then they might as well do it together.

"You're built," she mumbled, and she wiggled back just a fraction so she could put her hands between them and run them over his chest. “Really built,” she added, her voice soundless, all breath.

Parker was glad his body pleased her, because Bailey’s had the same effect on him. Well, what he could see of her body anyway.

“You have on too many clothes.” And he stripped off the stretchy pink top. Her bra was pink, too. Lace. Barely there. He could practically see her nipples through it, but *practically* wasn’t enough.

Parker kissed her neck and snapped open the front-close bra. Her breasts spilled into his hands. She was small, firm and perfect. And he kissed each of her breasts to let her know that. He lingered, to please himself, and circled her left nipple with his tongue.

She moaned. Arched her back, offering him a better position to take more. And just in case he hadn’t picked up on that little nonverbal signal, Bailey caught his hair and yanked him closer.

Oh, this was going to be a battle. Parker laughed. He didn’t care if this was one battle he lost.

He continued to kiss her breasts and neck, but he slid his hands to her bottom to lift her up so other parts of them could have some contact. Parker felt the fabric of her skirt and cursed.

“Still too many clothes,” he mumbled.

He shoved the skirt down her hips and to the floor, and he kicked it aside.

Her panties were pink lace, too.

“I like girlie underwear,” she mumbled when she saw him looking at her panties. She seemed almost embarrassed about that confession.

"So do I," he joked.

But the truth was, he would have been just as satisfied if she'd been wearing burlap. It wasn't the wrapping that got him hot. It was the woman beneath.

Parker shifted a little, so that he could bring her closer to him, but Bailey beat him to it. She hooked her long athletic right leg around the backs of his thighs and thrust him against her.

Her sex met his with perfect military precision. A frontal assault. The sensation was so overwhelming that it blurred his vision.

"Hell," he growled. Those panties were coming off now.

Without breaking the kiss or the sex contact, Parker lifted Bailey and carried her the few steps into the bedroom, and he dropped her onto the feather mattress. It swelled around her, partly cocooning her.

He managed to maneuver those lace barrier panties off her and himself nestled right between her legs.

Finally!

Bailey was naked, hot and kissing him as if…as if…

Parker quit trying to fill in the blanks. But he couldn't push aside that this felt different. Not just sex. Maybe something more.

And it couldn't be *more.*

Not as long as he was Bailey's bodyguard. He'd already broken enough rules without letting his heart have any say in this.

"Please tell me you have a condom," she whispered.

Did he?

Parker had a moment of near panic, but then he remembered during the move that he'd found a box and had put them in the nightstand drawer. He hadn't thought he'd ever use them, but he was thankful he was prepared. He nearly ripped off the drawer trying to get to one.

"I'll be too heavy for you," he murmured and tried to move her to another position.

"No way." Bailey held her ground, tightened the grip with her legs and put his sex right against hers. "I've been fantasizing about your body on mine, and it's going to happen now."

All right. He was too huge and too hard to argue with that. If she'd wanted sex on the kitchen table, Parker would have made it happen.

She lifted her hips at the same moment that Parker levered his down. Talk about a sweet collision. His vision blurred. His breath went who knows where. He didn't care. The only thing he could feel was being inside Bailey.

Hell. There was no way this would last very long. She was too tight, too wet and moving too fast as if she were already close to the edge.

Parker got her closer.

He thrust deep inside her. Again. Again. And again. Faster. And faster.

The sweat misted their bodies, making them slick.

Bailey dug her heels into the mattress, arching her entire body and making the union as complete as it could get. She made that sweet feminine sound, half moan, half plea.

"Finish me," she insisted.

That was exactly what he had in mind. He could make this unbearable heat burst. Could make the pleasure go off the scale.

So that's what Parker did.

He pushed into her one last time, and he felt her close around him. That was all he needed.

Just Bailey.

Parker surrendered.

His body went slack. So did his brain. And he had no idea how long it took him to find level ground again. Maybe ten minutes or more. All the primal, primitive urges inside him kept saying *satisfied, finished.* He'd taken the woman he wanted and had left his taste and scent on her.

But the truth was, Bailey had put her mark on him, as well.

He glanced down at her and realized he had to be crushing her. Even though Bailey had said she wanted him on top of her, he outweighed her by a good seventy pounds, and right now he was dead weight.

Hating that the intimate contact had to end, he rolled to the side and went into the bathroom. He wasn't gone long, less than a minute, but when he came back into the bedroom he was disappointed to see that Bailey had coiled the comforter around her. Maybe she was cold. The AC was blowing cold air from the overhead duct.

But she also looked a little uneasy.

Parker smiled, dropped down beside her and tried to defuse some of that uneasiness. "I finally got you in my bed."

"Yes."

He heard the hesitation in her voice and lifted his head slightly so he could look at her. She was staring at the scar on his shoulder.

Oh, *that*.

"Old wounds," he mumbled.

"There are three of them." Bailey touched her fingers to the one on his hip and sent a nice ripple of heat through that part of his body.

"All places where the bulletproof gear didn't cover me," he explained.

She bent down and brushed her mouth over it. More heat. Hell. He'd just had her. He couldn't want Bailey this much this soon.

"You got the wounds when you were protecting people?" she asked.

He heard the question, but then she switched positions, propping her elbow on his chest. The comforter shifted, and it gave him a really good view of her breasts.

"Yeah," he answered. And Parker leaned in and kissed her left nipple just as she'd done his scar.

She pulled in her breath and didn't release it for several seconds. The slight hitching sound she made was pure pleasure and revved him up all over again.

Yeah. He wanted her bad. And Parker would have sampled her other nipple if Bailey hadn't caught onto his face with her hands.

"If things turn ugly..." she whispered. Her voice was no longer hitching or filled with breath. "I don't want you to take a bullet for me."

He froze. "What?"

"I want you to think of Zach. You have to stay safe for him."

He didn't want to have this conversation. "I'm going to make sure both of you are safe. This isn't an either-or situation, Bailey."

She kissed him, hard and fast. "Just don't be a superhero for me. Save that for your son."

Oh, he would have argued with that, and Parker would have won, too. If the blasted doorbell hadn't rung. Since it could be the sheriff with an update, Parker jumped from the bed and began to locate his clothes. Bailey scrambled to do the same.

The doorbell rang again. This time it was followed by a heavy-handed knock.

"I'll be right there," Parker called out.

But the person rang the bell again. Parker pulled on a pair of clean jeans and a black T-shirt.

Bailey hurriedly put on her underwear and had her top halfway over her head when someone called out.

"Bailey? If you're in there, open up now," the man shouted.

"Oh, God." Bailey groaned. "It's Tim."

Parker cursed. This couldn't be good. He grabbed his gun off the dresser and headed for the door.

Chapter Eleven

Bailey pulled on her skirt and hurried after Parker. "Tim," she mumbled. Why the heck was he here?

She prayed nothing had happened to her mother.

Ahead of her, Parker disengaged the security system, and he unlocked and opened the door.

Tim was indeed there on the porch, his fist lifted, ready to knock again. But he wasn't alone. Her mother was by his side.

"What's wrong?" Bailey asked, rushing toward them.

"I was about to ask you the same thing," Lila countered. She combed her gaze over Bailey. Then over Parker.

Bailey silently groaned. There was no mirror around for her to check her appearance, but if she looked as rumpled as Parker did, then her mother had already guessed that Parker and she had just climbed out of bed.

A faint smile bent her mother's mouth, but it quickly faded. "The sheriff called and told me about the shooting here last night. It's sad that I heard it from him and not my own daughter. I considered calling you, but since you would probably just let it go to voice mail, I asked Tim to drive me out here. I wanted to see for myself that you were okay."

So, that's why she was here. Bailey had meant to call her, but she'd gotten distracted—first with her need for sleep and then her need for Parker. "I'm fine."

"We were worried about you," Tim snapped.

"I'm sorry," Bailey apologized. If she had to grovel, she would, but her first priority was getting them out of here. The longer her mother remained, the more speculation she would have about Parker and her.

Her mother pushed right past them and went inside.

Bailey huffed. So much for getting them to leave.

Tim stepped in as well, and Parker looked at Bailey as if he was trying to figure out how to handle this. Bailey just threw her hands in the air. Parker relented too because he finally just shut the door. And there they stood, all four of them, with the tension as thick as the muggy July heat outside.

It was obvious that Tim was upset about the call he'd received from Parker about the ruby ring. Tim glared at him. Her mother didn't glare exactly, but judging from what she'd said earlier, her feelings had apparently been hurt.

"Would you like to sit down?" Parker asked her mother, though it didn't sound like a heartfelt invitation.

Still, Lila took him up on it and sat on the sofa. Tim took the chair across from her. Since this was apparently going to turn into some kind of lecture, Bailey also sat on the sofa, but Parker stayed put, near the door, and he glanced out the window. He was the bodyguard even now.

"Bailey, I want you to come back to the ranch with us," her mother insisted.

Yes, definitely a lecture. "That's not a good idea. So far, this stalker seems to be after only me. It's been days since you've gotten a disgruntled letter. But me? Well, let's just say, this guy is trying to scare me, and I don't want to give him a reason to go to the ranch."

Lila crossed her arms. "Your safety is far more important than mine."

Bailey knew that her mother truly felt that way. She slid her hand over Lila's. "And I feel the same about you."

"Well, I don't want you to feel that way. I want my children safe, but I can't seem to make Chloe and you understand that."

"We do understand it, Mom. Devin has a bodyguard, too. Someone that Parker and Bart Bellows trust."

"Yes, I know. Bart called me. Devin did, too." Lila blinked back tears. "Someone shot at you, Bailey."

Bailey hated seeing her mother's tears, probably as much as her mother did. Lila wasn't a crier, so this was proof that she was truly upset and not just acting to get Bailey under her roof. She had to try to give her mother some peace of mind.

Even if she had to lie.

"The shots weren't meant to hurt me," Bailey explained. "They were purposely aimed at the stone on the exterior of the house. So, I'm not in any real danger. This stalker just wants to scare me."

Tim moved to the edge of his seat. "Do you really believe that?" He scrubbed his hand over his face. "Jesus H., Bailey, what does he have to do, put a gun to your head to make you realize you're in danger? Because you *are* in danger."

"He could be just trying to get some attention," Parker offered. "If he'd wanted to hurt Bailey, he could have fired into other parts of the house. He's had opportunities to do some real damage, but he's stuck with these juvenile scare tactics."

"Next time, this stalker might have a better aim," Tim snarled. His tone softened when he turned back to Bailey. "If you come to the ranch, I can protect you."

Tim reached across and caught onto her hand, as she'd done with her mother earlier. But Tim's touch felt clammy and, well…wrong. So Bailey pulled back, and Tim flinched as if she'd slapped him.

"I'm not blind," Tim snapped. "I can see what's going on between you and this so-called bodyguard. You're letting your emotions rule your actions, and that's not like you, Bailey. Trusting him could get you killed."

Her reaction was instant and intense. The anger raced through every vein in her body. "You have no idea what I'm like. And I trust Parker with my life." Bailey got to her feet, ready to toss Tim out.

Her mother got up as well, and Lila caught onto her shoulders. "We have your best interest at heart." Lila's voice was a lot calmer than Tim's, and she was obviously trying to defuse the tense situation.

"If that's true, then you'll leave and let Parker do his job." Bailey narrowed her eyes when she looked at Tim. "And I'm not going to be bullied by you or anyone else into going to the ranch."

"We're not trying to bully you," Tim insisted.

"That's what it feels like to me," Bailey fired back, "and since Mother does know me, she knows that this kind of demand will only make me dig in my heels. I'm not going anywhere."

Tim's mouth tightened, and he slid glances at both Parker and her. "Fine. He can come to the ranch, too. We can protect you together."

Since Tim gave Bailey the creeps, that wasn't exactly a good offer, and her expression must have conveyed that because her mother sighed.

"Come on, Tim," Lila said. "We're wasting our breaths and time." She looked at Parker. "Please keep her safe."

"I will." And Parker didn't hesitate. "But I do have some questions—about the threats you've received, Governor Lockhart."

Lila stiffened a little. "What about them?"

"I've been told bits and pieces, but I haven't actually read any of the letters. The one that Chester Herman threw out of his car for Bailey said 'This isn't over. Hope you enjoy what I have planned for you.' Is that the same tone as yours?"

"No." Lila seemed surprised by that because she put her hand to her chest and repeated the *no*. "The threats, if you can call them that, say things like—vote this way on a particular bill or you'll be sorry. There isn't a mocking tone. In fact, if the person had actually signed the letters, I might not have even considered them threats but rather just an annoyed constituent voicing an opinion."

"But he didn't sign them," Tim pointed out. "And coupled with several hang-up calls from a prepaid untraceable cell phone, there's a reason for concern. I'm worried about both of them," Tim went on. "I've added some extra security at the ranch, and I've been studying the footage from the surveillance cameras. Early this morning, I saw some guy near the fence. He looked just like Sidney Burrell."

That obviously got Parker's attention. He walked closer. "You called Sheriff Hale?"

Tim shook his head. "The guy was dressed like a hunter, and I figured he'd be long gone before the sheriff got out there. Besides, if he'd gotten onto the property, I would have shot first and asked questions later." He looked at Parker. "How about the guy in your yard last night? You think that was Sidney?"

"Maybe."

Bailey wondered why Parker hadn't volunteered that it could have been their other suspect, Chester Herman, but she didn't question it.

Lila's phone rang. "Business," she commented, glancing at the screen. "And I have to take this call. Tim, I'll meet you in the car."

Lila mumbled her goodbyes, gave Bailey a kiss on the cheek and walked out. Parker kept the door open, waiting for Tim to leave, as well.

But he didn't. Tim stood and stared at Bailey. "I'd like a word with you *alone*."

Bailey glanced at Parker to see what he thought of that. Oh, he wanted to object, but he wouldn't. He would allow her to make her own decision about this. At first, Bailey's decision was a big fat *No!* but she rethought that. She did want to ask Tim about that ring to see if he would give her the same tidy answer he'd given Parker.

"I'll be outside on the porch," Parker explained. "I won't be far, just a few steps away." And he aimed that warning at Tim.

Tim didn't say a word until Parker was indeed outside, and then he moved closer to Bailey. "I think you're making a mistake," Tim whispered.

Bailey folded her arms over her chest. "A mistake? You mean similar to one the jeweler made on the ring you ordered for Mom? For the record, rubies aren't her style. She's more of a diamonds-and-pearls person. I, on the other hand, have several pieces of ruby jewelry and anyone who knows me knows that it's my favorite gemstone."

Whatever he'd been expecting her to say, that wasn't it. He looked a little poleaxed, and it took Tim several seconds to regain his composure.

"The ring wasn't for you," he insisted. "I ordered it for your mother, and the jeweler made a mistake, that's all. Parker blew this situation out of proportion so that you wouldn't trust me."

"Why would he do that?" she fired back.

"Maybe because he's jealous of me."

Bailey gave him a flat stare.

A stare that put some fire in Tim's eyes. "Or maybe Parker just wants to create trouble. The point is the ring was a mistake, but it can be fixed. The jeweler can add the other two names. Your situation can be fixed too, Bailey. I can fix things for you."

She groaned. "By coming to the ranch?" Bailey didn't wait for him to confirm that. "No, thanks. I'm staying here with Parker."

"Parker," he repeated like a profanity. "It's obvious that he wants you. You're a wealthy woman, Bailey. The governor's daughter. He's got a mortgage on this house. He's not your kind of people."

"Excuse me?" The anger sliced through her. "What does that mean—*your kind of people?* If it weren't for my trust fund, I'd have a mortgage too, and I'd be in debt up to my eyeballs for all those renovations to the day care." She shook her head. "Why are we even discussing this? Parker's net worth is none of our business."

Tim caught onto her arm, but she threw off his grip. "It is my business, because I care about you. About Lila and her entire family," he quickly added.

She got in his face. "You were hired to protect my mother, that's all. Now, while I'm very happy that you've done an excellent job as her bodyguard, you are *not* part of my life. Never have been, never will be."

Bailey hadn't intended to be so harsh, but she wanted to make it clear that she had no interest in him. Plus, she was furious at what he'd said about Parker.

Tim backed away from her, each step slow and calculated. "As long as I work for your mother, I'll always be part of her life. And yours."

It sounded like a threat. His tight jaw muscles added to the menacing feel.

"I would have died for you," Tim tossed at her, and he stormed out, leaving her to stand there and wonder what the heck had just happened.

When she heard Parker talking, Bailey hurried out to the porch. She thought that Tim might be starting round two with Parker, and she wanted to nip it in the bud. But Tim was already in the limo, and he and her mother were driving away. Parker, however, was speaking to someone on the phone.

"Bailey and I will be there in ten minutes," Parker said to the caller, and he snapped his phone shut.

Oh, mercy. What had gone wrong now?

"That was Sheriff Hale," Parker informed her. "He found Chester Herman."

She felt both the fear and relief. "Where is he?" *Please, don't let him be near Zach.*

"At the sheriff's office."

The relief got a lot stronger. "Sheriff Hale has him in custody?"

"Not exactly. Chester walked in a few minutes ago and said he wanted to talk. To you and me. He said we'd be very interested in what he has to tell us."

Chapter Twelve

Parker stepped around the eight-foot-high inflatable Uncle Sam so he could open the heavy glass door to the sheriff's office. Main Street was a hive of activity with the work crews stringing red, white and blue streamers and lights for tomorrow's Fourth of July parade.

The air felt festive.

Parker felt some of that, too. Judging from the way she was smiling and greeting people, so did Bailey. The sheriff finally had their number one suspect off the streets and in custody. If Sheriff Hale could make the stalking charges stick, Chester Herman would be arrested, and Bailey could reopen Cradles to Crayons and get on with her life.

Parker wanted that for her. He wanted her safe and at work at the job she loved. But he kept going back to one question.

What now?

Bart Bellows had told Parker that he would remain in Freedom so that Zach would have some stability, but Parker also knew there was a likelihood that future jobs with Corps Security and Investigations would take him out of town.

And away from Bailey.

Even if there was work for him in Freedom, that didn't mean Parker would see her often. It was possible their paths wouldn't cross again.

"Something wrong?" Bailey asked.

Parker pulled himself out of his little trance and realized then that even though he'd opened the door of the sheriff's office for her, he hadn't budged. He was just standing there, probably with a blank look on his face. That got him moving, and Bailey and he made their way past a dispatch/reception desk and to Sheriff Hale's office. The sheriff wasn't there, however. He was in the small interrogation room across the hall.

So was Chester Herman.

The sheriff and Chester weren't alone though. Sidney Burrell was seated at the metal table across from them. There were no lawyers, so maybe that meant both men were ready to talk.

Bailey and Parker didn't join them at the table. There were extra chairs, but Parker didn't want her any closer to either of the men, so they continued to stand.

"Two for the price of one," Sheriff Hale commented. "Sidney here walked in a couple of minutes ago and wanted to talk, too. Must be the day for confessions and conversation, huh?"

"I didn't know he'd be here," Sidney practically growled, and he aimed his index finger at Chester. "He's your suspect. Not me. I'm just a guy with a juvenile record who's getting railroaded."

"Hold your horses," the sheriff growled back. "Nobody's accused you of anything—yet."

"Tell that to the people in this narrow-minded town," Sidney answered. "I can't get a job and got no money to move. I'm stuck here, and the only chance I got is to clear my name."

Chester smiled. It was as cocky as the rest of his demeanor. A well-chewed toothpick dangled from his chapped mouth. "My feelings would be hurt if y'all were accusing me of anything."

Parker glared at him. He had no intention of playing games with this moron. "You threw a threatening letter into the parking lot of the day care that Bailey owns," Parker reminded him.

"Oh, *that*." Chester smiled again. "I didn't know it was threatening. It was folded up, and I didn't even read it."

"Sure, you didn't." Parker stepped closer.

"I didn't," Chester insisted, though he didn't look the least bit concerned that he was being accused of stalking. "Yesterday morning when I went out to my mailbox, that folded-up piece of paper was there, with a note and half of a hundred-dollar bill paper-clipped to it. The note was addressed to me and said I was to leave the folded piece of paper in the day care building parking lot, after I sat there a spell. If I did that, I'd get the other half of the hundred."

"Who left the paper in your mailbox?" Bailey asked, taking the question right out of Parker's mouth.

"Don't have a clue."

Chester's flippant response created stares and grumbles from the rest of them, especially Sidney.

"I want the note and the half of the hundred-dollar bill," the sheriff ordered. "I want to test it for prints."

"Didn't keep the note. The bill is at my house, but I got to warn you, I accidentally left it in my jeans pocket, and I ran it through the washer. Bleached the daylights out of it." He chuckled about that.

"Did this anonymous person pay you the other half of the hundred when the *errand* was done?" Parker wanted to know.

"No." Chester dropped the smile. "That's why I came here. I don't mind running a few errands for people, but if you promise to give me money for my services and then renege, there'll be hell to pay. I think Sidney might be the one who catches that hell."

"I had no part in this." Sidney got to his feet and loomed over Chester. "And I damn sure didn't offer you any money to do anything."

Chester didn't appear intimidated. He stared up at Sidney and shrugged. "So says you, but it's all over town that you got your dander up when Miz Lockhart here fired your sorry butt. I figure you wanted to get back at her, and you used me to do it. Well, guess what—I'm not taking the blame for low-life scum like you."

Parker studied both men whose reactions and emotions seemed sincere. *Seemed.* But he wasn't about to trust appearances.

"You two went to school together," Parker pointed out. "So, is this argument all an act?"

Both Chester and Sidney snapped their attention to Parker.

"Why would I do something like that?" Sidney demanded.

"Because as long as you're pointing accusing fingers at the other, then it muddies the water of who's really guilty," Parker explained. "Heck, maybe you both are."

Chester's eyes darkened. "I wouldn't work with the likes of him. He's a woman beater, you know that? Beat the crud out of his girl back in school." He shook his head. "Only a coward hits a woman with his fists, and that's what you are—a coward."

A feral sound tore from Sidney's throat, and he dove at Chester. Parker pushed Bailey out of the way and caught onto Chester when the man moved in Sidney's direction. Sheriff Hale latched onto Sidney's shoulder and slammed him back into his seat. Parker did the same to Chester.

"You get up again," the sheriff warned both men, "and I'll arrest you for disturbing the peace, attempted assault and any other charges I can think up. Got that?"

"Yeah. I got that." Sidney's anger was evident in every part of his body, especially his eyes. He aimed venomous glares at Bailey and Parker.

Chester just seemed amused by it all. If this was act, it was a good one.

"So, let me get this straight," the sheriff said, his drawl calm and easy despite having just broken up a fight. "You two aren't working together. Both of you claim you're so innocent that I'm surprised I don't see halos circling around your knot-hard heads. But last night somebody rigged a gun with a silencer to shoot into Parker McKenna's house. And I'm thinking one of you two saints did that."

"Not me," Chester piped up.

"Darn sure not me," Sidney concurred.

Bailey huffed, and Parker felt every bit of her frustration. The sheriff just shook his head and mumbled some profanity. He added an apologetic murmur to Bailey for using the Lord's name in vain in front of her.

"Why did you drive the black car around Bailey's neighborhood and in front of the day care?" Parker asked Chester.

Chester lifted his shoulder. "Somebody left me money and another note in my mailbox. Not half of a hundred, but the whole thing. The note said to use part of it for gas to drive around. So, that's what I did. I drove around and used the rest of it to buy some barbecued ribs and beer over at Jo-Jo's. Last I heard that wasn't a crime, neither."

Parker bracketed his hands on the table and got right in Chester's face. "You expect us to believe you weren't stalking Bailey?"

"I wasn't." Chester motioned around the room. "You think I would have come here if I thought Sheriff Hale had any reason to arrest me? I've done nothing wrong other than buying a car with bogus plates, which, by the way, I've already worked out with the Department of Motor Vehicles. And, of course, there's that littering citation the sheriff gave me, but I'm here to pay the fine for that."

Chester took out his wallet. "The fine for littering is steep. Don't Mess with Texas," he joked, repeating the phrase used on many road signs. He pulled out five one-hundred-dollar bills from his wallet and slapped them on the table. One had been torn in half and then put back together with tape.

Parker wanted to punch this moron so bad he could taste it. "Let me guess. Your secret employer gave you that to pay your fine."

"No. That was birthday money from my mama. I accidentally tore the bill and had to fix it." The oily smile returned in full force.

"He's guilty," Sidney spat out. "Arrest him."

"Careful," Chester warned Sidney. "Or you might be the one to land in jail. You know ol' Sheriff Hale will do anything Lila Lockhart tells him to do, and I'll bet Lila's pushing hard to arrest somebody, *anybody*." Chester paused. "Especially since it could be the governor herself who's doing all this."

"What?" Bailey practically shouted.

Chester's expression didn't change. "Just think about it. All this fuss, and you're not really in any danger. But you and your family, including your mama, are getting a lot of sympathy. Now, if she weren't a politician, I'd say no big deal, but we all know she's gonna make a run for president. What better way to start than to get a whole bunch of free publicity?"

"That's absurd," Parker insisted.

Chester shrugged again. "Believe what you will, but just this morning I was reading in the paper about how the governor's approval rating is up. Sympathy can get her a lot of votes."

"I've heard enough of this," Bailey mumbled and started for the door.

"Listen to him," Sidney spoke up, "because somebody is doing this stuff to you, and it's not me."

"Well, it's not my mother." Bailey stormed out and into the hall.

Parker followed her. "I'm sorry."

Bailey waved him off, but the wave did nothing to calm the tension in her face. "I should have known Chester would try to put the blame on anyone but himself. Coming here was a waste of time."

Maybe. But Parker had learned more about the potential enemy. Before this little chat, he'd thought that maybe Sidney and Chester were working together.

Parker didn't think that now.

There was too much distrust and animosity between the two men. And there was Chester's hatred for Sidney's assault on a woman. Chester was cold and callous, but that anger toward Sidney was real.

And that brought Parker back to the allegations Chester had made against Lila. They were probably nonsense.

Probably.

But he made a mental note to do some checking. Lila truly seemed to love her children, and Bart trusted her. However, it wouldn't hurt to make a few inquiries.

"You believed him," he heard Bailey say. She was staring at him as if she could read his mind.

"No," he tried to assure her, but he obviously wasn't very convincing, because Bailey started for the door.

Parker turned to go after her, but the sheriff stepped out of the interrogation room.

"Just so you know, I'll keep both of them for an hour or two," Sheriff Hale explained, "but I got no grounds to hold them any longer."

Parker cursed. This was not what he wanted to hear, but he had known it was coming. The sheriff could have possibly held Chester if he hadn't cleared up that littering citation and the bogus plates on his car. But he had fixed those things. And as for Sidney—well, there was no proof of any current wrongdoing.

"I'll cut them loose and then have one of the deputies follow them," the sheriff continued. "I can't tie up all my men though. Not with the big parade tomorrow."

This was a critical conversation, but Parker kept checking on Bailey. He had to talk to her. "Bart Bellows might be able to help. I'll call Corps headquarters and get someone over here to tail them both."

That would take care of Chester and Sidney, but Parker didn't have a clue how he was going to handle the possible situation with Lila.

Parker thanked the sheriff and went after Bailey. This was about to get ugly.

Chapter Thirteen

Bailey felt as if she were moving in slow motion. Everything was off-kilter, especially her mood, and she doubted that would improve anytime soon unless she got off this emotional roller coaster that she had been on for days.

At least in the past twenty-four hours no one had stalked her, slashed her tires, shot at a house where she was staying or left her menacing notes. That was something, but it was a sad testament to her life nonetheless.

She finished her shower and dressed in a red cotton dress, the only clean outfit she had left in her suitcase. She put on her makeup and stared at herself in the mirror.

What was she going to do?

After Chester Herman's outlandish accusations against her mother the day before at the sheriff's office, Bailey had seen the flash of doubt in Parker's eyes. Maybe it was little more than a passing consideration, but the point was, Parker had *considered* that her mother might have been responsible for the threats. She wasn't.

Her mother might be domineering, but Lila loved her children.

Bailey cursed and tossed her makeup back into her cosmetics bag.

Yesterday, Bailey had the best sex of her entire life, but after that visit with Chester, they had hardly spoken, and Bailey had slept in the guest room last night—alone.

It riled her to think of how easily Parker had accepted the sleeping arrangements. He darn sure hadn't argued when she'd told him that was her plan. Where was the invitation to his bed? And why hadn't he come to her to try to work things out?

She cursed again.

Why hadn't she gone to him?

Because his doubts had hurt her to the core, that's why. Still, after a restless night's sleep and an equally restless morning, Bailey was seeing things in a new light.

And her heart was breaking.

Bailey had done exactly what she had sworn she wouldn't do. She had fallen hard for the hot GI who wasn't emotionally available. She should admit it—when it came to men, her judgment just plain sucked.

With the battle still going on inside her, she threw open the bathroom door and ran face-first into Parker.

He caught her in his arms but then quickly let go and stepped back. Way back. In fact, he leaned against the wall, as far away from her as he could get. He had that look on his face. The we-need-to-talk look, and he was probably going to verbalize the conclusion that she had already reached—that sex had been a mistake.

A mistake that had felt great.

But a mistake nonetheless.

"I know what you want to say." Bailey went for a preemptive strike. "You're breaking up with me. Except it's not an actual breakup, I suppose, since we never went out on a date."

Parker blinked. "I just wanted to say I'm sorry." His forehead bunched up. "You thought I was going to break up with you?"

"You weren't?" just flew right out of her mouth.

"No," said in the same tone as *when pigs fly*.

She studied his expression to make sure this was no breakup. And Bailey suddenly felt a little stupid. "Well, we haven't exactly been on speaking terms in the past twenty-four hours."

He nodded, stuffed his hands into the pockets of his jeans and leaned the back of his head against the wall. "I wanted to give you some time. I know I upset you when I doubted your mother's innocence." He paused, made eye contact with her. "I don't have a good track record when it comes to trusting people. I just wanted to make sure I was doing everything to keep you safe."

"I know." And she did know that, but it stung. "Are you still suspicious of my mother?"

"No. The other things—the slashed tires, the note and the vandalized office—those were situations where you couldn't have been hurt. But the bullets could have done some damage. You could have been killed. Plus, your mother has an alibi for the night your office was vandalized. Bart was at the ranch with her, and they stayed up late talking until the early hours of the morning."

"So, that's what you've been doing," she mumbled. Checking her mother's alibis. Bailey hated that he'd even had to do that, but she was glad that her mother was no longer a suspect in Parker's mind.

She was also glad there was no breakup.

Of course, that didn't eliminate the obstacles between her and Parker. There were plenty of things that could get in their way. Like Zach. Parker's feelings for his late wife. Bailey's bizarre family.

Oh, and the fact that she was in danger from a psycho stalker who had put Parker's son in harm's way.

Yes, that was a biggie.

Bailey stared at him, and for a just a moment, she could forget the obstacles and the danger. Parker was a tasty morsel, all right, in his jeans and snug T-shirt that showed off his body. She was familiar with that body now. She'd had her hands and mouth all over him, and that one time with him had only left her wanting more.

Like now, for instance.

"I've also been on the computer or phone," Parker explained. "Lots of security issues to work out."

Bailey heard what he said, but her mind was already starting to spin a fantasy. One where she kissed him and dragged him to the floor.

She felt herself blush and then reminded herself that just minutes earlier she had considered a breakup between them to be a good thing. There was still a possibility that Parker was not yet over his wife's death.

But he hadn't mentioned Amy recently.

Of course, that didn't mean he wasn't thinking about his wife right now, while he was looking at her. Heaven knows the kind of guilt trip he'd put himself through. Yes, the sex had been amazing, but now both Parker and she were dealing with the aftermath and consequences.

She huffed.

That didn't stop her from wanting him all over again.

"Did you hear me?" Parker asked.

Uh, no, she hadn't. Her expression must have conveyed that, too. Hopefully, it hadn't conveyed anything else that she'd been thinking.

"I said I hope you weren't planning to go into town for the parade." Parker said it slowly and cautiously as if she might argue. "It starts in less than an hour."

Yes. That was indeed today. Bailey loved Freedom's Independence Day parade. It was one of her favorite things, right up there with the Christmas lights on Main Street and the annual Easter-egg hunt in the city park.

But she understood his concern.

"You'll be able to see some of it from the front porch," Parker explained. "The floats will pass by at the end of the street, and I can even tap in to the traffic camera on my laptop if you want a closer look."

She nodded. "It won't be the same…." But then, not much was the same these days.

"Good." And after a deep breath, Parker repeated it.

"I wish I could talk your mother and sister into staying home, as well."

Bailey was still looking at him as if he were a box of premium chocolates, but that got her attention. "Excuse me?"

"Your mother and Chloe. They're both insisting that they go to the parade."

"What? Have their lost their minds? That would be the perfect place for a stalker to strike." She'd put her phone in her dress pocket, and she couldn't get it out fast enough. She tried Chloe's number first. "Her bodyguard couldn't talk her out of this?"

"No. And he tried, trust me. I was worried that you'd demand to go, too."

A few days ago, she would have demanded. Correction: she would have gone to the parade. But things were different now. If she went, so would Parker, and she wasn't a fool. Both of them would be in danger. She didn't want to put Zach's dad at risk because she was stubborn. It just wasn't that important.

"Chloe's call went to voice mail," Bailey mumbled. Her sister had likely done that on purpose because Chloe would have known why Bailey was calling and probably wanted to avoid an argument.

"I spoke to Harlan McClain less than a half hour ago," Parker assured her. "He'll stay right beside her." He placed his fingers beneath her chin and gently lifted it to look in her eyes. "Harlan is former black ops. He can handle a stalker and Chloe. Plus, there have been no threats of any kind made to your sister."

Bailey knew he was right, and she also knew she

stood zero chance of changing Chloe's mind. Her sister was stubborn, just like the rest of their family.

Especially their mother.

"Mom doesn't have a black-ops bodyguard," Bailey pointed out. "She has Tim." And since Bailey wasn't sure she could even trust him, she pressed her mother's number next.

When Lila answered, Bailey put the call on speaker.

"Did something happen?" her mother immediately asked.

"No. Not yet anyway. But I just found out you're going to the parade."

"Of course I am. I've been the grand marshal of the Freedom parade for the last eleven years. Nothing's changed."

"Everything has changed," Bailey reminded her. "You've been threatened."

"Just letters, Bailey. There has been nothing even remotely dangerous. You are the one I'm worried about so I called Parker this morning. He assured me that he'd do everything possible short of hog-tying you to keep you away from the parade."

Bailey looked up at Parker who only shrugged. He obviously wasn't going to apologize for doing his job.

"I'll be fine," her mother continued. "I spoke to Bart a couple minutes ago, and he's sending out several of his men to shadow me."

That gave Bailey some relief. Tim wouldn't be the only one guarding her, but that didn't eliminate all her worries. "It would be better if you stayed at the ranch. Or you can come here and watch from the porch with me."

"Thanks for the generous offer, but I'm going to the parade. I'm already in town, waiting at the sheriff's office. Besides, I couldn't get to Parker's house except on foot. The streets have already been closed so the crews can do the final decorations."

True. For most of Independence Day, downtown Freedom wasn't accessible by car, and all the shops were closed. Bailey definitely didn't want her mother walking the half mile or so from where she would have to park.

"Mother, just promise me that you'll stay with Bart's men or the sheriff until the parade is over and you get back to the ranch."

"I promise, if you'll give me your word that you won't leave Parker's side."

That sounded a little sexual, even though she knew her mother hadn't meant it that way. Perhaps that's because Bailey still had sex on the brain when it came to Parker.

"Deal," Bailey promised. "I love you, Mom."

"Oh, Bailey, I love you, too." And her mother sounded so surprised that Bailey made a mental note to tell her more often. Because she did indeed love her mother, and she prayed this day would end with her family safe and sound.

"I tried," Bailey said to Parker when she ended the call. "Now, what about Zach? I suppose he's going to the parade, too?"

Parker nodded. "But he'll be with Josh and his dad,

and they're going to watch from the street in front of the sheriff's office. Zach said when he goes to any of the food booths, Josh will go with him."

Good. That was one less worry.

And one less thing for them to discuss.

The silence that followed settled uncomfortably between them.

Bailey was about to tell Parker that she was sorry for the silent treatment she'd given him the day before. She was also sorry that things weren't going so well between them. She needed to remind him of her track record with men, and then he could tell her all about how complicated his life was.

But she didn't get to say any of those things.

That's because Parker leaned down and kissed her.

It was so unexpected that the gesture alone nearly robbed her of her breath. What little air she managed to hang on to evaporated because of the heat of the kiss.

How could he do that?

With just the merest touch of his mouth against hers, Parker could make her forget all her doubts and all the valid arguments that should keep them apart.

"Do we need to discuss this?" he asked, his mouth still touching hers.

Bailey moved back just a fraction so she could consider that. "Discussing it would be the smart thing to do," she admitted. "But kissing would be a lot more fun."

Parker smiled, briefly. "I know the argument we should have. I've already had it with myself. The bottom line is I'm losing objectivity when it comes to you, and that's not a good thing."

Bailey couldn't dispute that. She had lost objectivity too, and that meant she couldn't tell if this relationship should end or if they should just shut up and, well, kiss, and deal with the aftermath later.

It was a potentially painful aftermath.

She already had deep feelings for Parker. Feelings that would no doubt give her another broken heart. Kissing him or having sex with him again certainly wouldn't do anything to lessen those feelings.

"Decisions, decisions," she mumbled.

But Bailey went with the kiss.

She slid her hand around the back of his neck and pulled him down to her. Parker didn't disappoint, but this kiss wasn't rough and ravenous like the other ones that had landed them in his bed. No. He was gentle and kissed her as if she were delicate fragile glass that might shatter in his hands.

Bailey had thought that the slow gentleness would cause her body to go in that direction, as well. But she had a hunger for him that just didn't seem capable of being filled.

Not for long anyway.

And it didn't take much of the kiss to spin her out of control. Bailey felt her body give way. She didn't even care. That should have been a gigantic red flag, but all she could think of was wanting, and having, Parker.

"Bailey," he warned.

He caught onto her shoulders, opened his mouth and would have no doubt started the argument that he'd already said they should have. But Bailey put a stop to that.

"I'm sure," she promised. "In fact, I've never been more sure of anything."

She studied his eyes. Cursed. And the argument didn't happen, even though Bailey hadn't exactly told the truth. Yes. She was sure about having sex with Parker, but she knew that eventually they would have issues to deal with.

But for now, Parker kissed her and slipped his arm around her waist. He lifted her and deepened the kiss. That revved up her heartbeat, and she could taste it along with Parker himself. The adrenaline and the heat sliding together, the same way was his body slid against hers.

Her arms came around him. She had to get closer, and it had to happen now. But Parker still held back. He kept things gentle when she was giving him all kinds of nonverbal cues to makes things happen hard and fast.

As if nothing was urgent, especially the fire roaring inside her, Parker started moving her toward his bedroom. Along the way, Bailey kissed his neck, his ear, and he made a maddening male sound when she flicked her tongue over the spot just below his ear.

So, she kissed him there.

It was the way to speed things up, all right. Parker groaned, and his grip on her tightened. He kissed her hard, just the way she wanted. It felt just on the rim of being dangerous, and it made her even hotter.

She kissed that spot below his ear again. And again.

Parker's cursing got worse, and he called her name that had her smiling with this newly found power. Turn about was fair play. If he could drive her crazy, she could do the same to him.

They made it as far as his bedroom door, and the cursing stopped. He dragged her to the floor, pulling at her clothes. Bailey pulled at his too but finally gave up. She wanted too much too fast to bother getting naked.

Parker had already maneuvered her dress up to her hips, and she hooked her thumb onto her panties to shimmy them off her. Parker unzipped his jeans and freed his huge erection from his boxers. Bailey didn't wait a second before she thrust her hips forward and took him inside her.

Her vision blurred. Her breath vanished. And every nerve in her body was humming and begging for this man. How could something feel this good?

How could she want someone this much?

Parker began to move inside her, and she no longer cared about questions. Or answers. Or anything else. The only thing she could see and feel was Parker.

He wasn't gentle now, and that was good. Later, they could go to bed and spoon and do all those other things that lovers did, but for now, Bailey wanted release. She wanted him to take her to that higher peak.

And then let her go.

"Parker," she managed to say, hoping it let him know that she was close to that peak. He knew how to take her the rest of way. She was sure of it. Parker seemed to know every secret of her body.

He moved harder. Faster. Deeper. And he just kept

moving until everything inside her shattered. She came in a flash narrowing to that one moment.

To that one man.

Bailey was too far gone to tell him that he was exactly what she wanted, exactly what she needed. She simply hung on. Until he released her.

And himself.

Bailey knew what was coming next. The crash and burn. She couldn't move, couldn't level her breathing. She could only lie beneath him with what had to be a really stupid grin on her face.

She gathered enough breath to kiss him and was about to tell him how special this was, but he lifted his head and looked down at her. His eyes were huge. His mouth dropped open.

"I didn't use a condom," Parker announced.

Oh, heck.

Well, that took care of her post-climatic high.

Bailey forced herself not to panic. She had to think, and she tried to do the math. Oh, mercy.

She was useless at math.

"It's the fourth of the month," Parker supplied. He'd obviously figured out where her mind was going.

"The fourth," she repeated, and she thought back to the date of her last cycle. Only a week ago. "We're okay," she assured. "It's the wrong time of the month."

She was relieved. And then she ruined the relief by considering a truly harebrained idea.

So what if she got pregnant?

She desperately wanted children, and truth was, she had decided if she wasn't in a serious relationship within the next six months or so, she would use artificial insemination to have a baby. She had already visited a clinic and gotten information about the process. So, this wasn't something to dread.

Except it might be for Parker.

He was staring at her. Apparently waiting for her to speak.

"It's okay," she assured him. "Even if I got pregnant, I wouldn't expect anything from you."

His mouth closed. And then tightened. His eyes narrowed, too. Parker rolled off her and landed hard on his back on the floor. Cursing the whole time, he fixed his jeans and his shirt.

"Well, you sure as hell should expect something. I dragged you to the floor, Bailey, and I had sex with you. If I got you pregnant, I'm not just going to walk away."

All right. That wasn't a declaration of love or marriage, but she hadn't expected that anyway. She was still working out how she felt about him.

"It's the wrong time of the month," she repeated. She hesitated, wondering if she should press this. What the heck. She hadn't exactly been the model of propriety here. "Do you want other children?"

Parker stayed silent for several seconds and then groaned. "Yes, I do. Very much so. And I know what you're thinking. How could he possibly want more kids when he can't handle the one he's got."

"I wasn't thinking that at all." Bailey rolled to her side so she could see his face and was about to tell what she was indeed thinking.

But the ringing shot through the hall and caused Parker to come up off the floor.

It was the house phone, and Parker started toward the nightstand to answer it. He didn't make it in time because on the second ring, his answering machine turned on. The person didn't leave a message. They hung up, and moments later his cell phone rang.

Oh, no.

This couldn't be good, so she got up, as well. She tried not to leap to conclusions, but Bailey glanced at the screen on his phone.

And her heart went to her knees.

The call was coming from the Holy Cross Hospital emergency room.

Chapter Fourteen

Parker stabbed the button to answer the call. "Parker McKenna," he managed to say, though his own heartbeat was right in his throat.

"I'm a nurse at Holy Cross E.R.," the woman said. Her voice was shaky, filled with nerves. "I tried your home phone, but I just got the answering machine. I didn't want to leave a message because I had to speak to you immediately."

"What's wrong?" Parker held his breath. Bailey was beside him now, and she was doing the same.

"There's been an accident," the nurse explained, "and your son, Zach, was hurt. He was apparently watching the parade and slipped underneath a float. It rolled over him, and he's en route to the hospital now."

Parker tried to say something, anything, but he couldn't. The phone would have fallen from his hand if Bailey hadn't latched onto it. She pushed the speaker function.

"How bad?" Parker finally said.

"I'm sorry to tell you this, Mr. McKenna, but according to the medics in the ambulance, it's very bad. We need you here at the hospital right away to sign some papers so we can get Zach in for surgery the moment he arrives. If it doesn't happen soon, he's not going to make it. Zach's condition is critical."

"I'm on the way."

Everything inside Parker started to whirl around like a tornado. All the bad memories of Amy's accident. He'd lost a child that day, too, and his life had been changed forever because of that loss. He couldn't lose Zach.

He couldn't lose his son.

"I can't use the car because the roads are closed," Parker mumbled, forcing himself to think. He had to get to Zach now, and he didn't want to take the time to have the sheriff clear the streets.

"You'll have to go on foot to the sheriff's office," Bailey explained. "If you run, it won't take you more than fifteen minutes. Just cut through the greenbelt at the back of the house and you can run to Main Street. It'll be packed because of the parade, but you can get to the sheriff who can use an emergency vehicle on the back roads. You'll make it to the hospital in time."

In time.

He prayed that was true. Amy had died before she could even get into surgery, but that's because it had taken too long to get her from the crushed car and into an ambulance. Zach was already on the way to the hospital.

Parker hurried to the kitchen and the back door but then stopped.

Bailey.

What was he going to do with her?

He didn't want her in the middle of Main Street with hundreds of people around. That would be the perfect place for the stalker to launch another attack.

"I'll be all right *here,*" Bailey assured him. "Just go. I'll lock the door and arm the security system. What's the code?"

Parker told her but then shook his head. "That's not enough. I need to call Bart to get someone out here to keep watch."

"I'll call him. Just get to Zach." She punched in the code into the wall keypad, threw open the door and practically shoved him out onto the porch.

Still, Parker hesitated. Yes, he had to get to the hospital, but he was worried about Bailey.

"Go!" she demanded. And she gave him another shove.

The nurse's words slammed through Parker much harder than the push that Bailey gave him.

Zach's condition is critical.

There was no time to wait for a replacement to arrive. No time to take any other security precautions. He just prayed that his son would make it through this and that the stalker wasn't anywhere near his house.

"The combination lock for the gun cabinet above the fridge is eight-four-six-two," Parker told her. "Take out the handgun. It's already loaded. Keep it with you until Bart can get someone else out here."

"I will, I promise. Now, go!" Bailey slammed the door shut, and the moment Parker heard her lock it, he raced off the porch and toward the greenbelt.

He had to get his son *fast.*

BAILEY'S HANDS WERE SHAKING when she reset the security alarm. This couldn't be happening. Fate couldn't be this cruel, again.

The thought of Zach being hurt sickened her. Neither Parker nor he deserved to go through this, and she prayed the surgery would save Zach's life. Not just for Zach but for Parker. It would destroy him to lose his son.

It took her several seconds to tamp down her thoughts just so she could move. She had things to do, to make sure she stayed safe. Bailey certainly didn't want Parker worrying about her at a time like this.

First, she called Corps Security headquarters. No answer. Of course there wouldn't be. It was a holiday. Her call was routed to an answering service, and Bailey left a message for Bart to call her.

With that ticked off her mental list, Bailey used the combination that Parker had given her for the gun cabinet and took out the handgun. She checked. Yes, it was loaded, but she prayed she didn't have to use it. There had already been enough bad in this day without adding anything else. To think—just a half hour earlier, she'd been counting her blessings for such a quiet morning.

And speaking of quiet, it was literally *quiet*. Except for her own heartbeat drumming in her ears. It didn't take long though for that quietness to close in around her, and Bailey started to pace. She had to do something to help.

But what?

Bailey took out her phone and stared at it. She glanced at the house phone, too. Both silent. Of course, it was much too soon for Parker or even Bart to call. Parker had probably just now made it to Main Street, and even though he was no doubt running as fast as he could, heaven knew how long it would take him to cut through the crowd and then get to the sheriff's office.

"The sheriff," Bailey mumbled.

She could call Sheriff Hale, and if he didn't know already, she could tell him what was going on and then ask him to help clear a path for Parker. He could have the emergency vehicle ready to go if it wasn't already.

Bailey pressed the button to begin the call and saw the two words.

No Service.

That was strange. She'd had service earlier when she called Corps Security headquarters.

She hurried into the doorway of the bathroom where she'd made that call, and the message on her cell's screen stayed the same: No Service. There were cell service dead spots all over Freedom and the surrounding area, but this was a first for her to experience it in Parker's house.

Since the house phone was a landline, Bailey ran back to the kitchen to use it. She could call 9-1-1-and reach the sheriff or one of the deputies that way. But the moment she took the phone from the wall, she realized it, too, was silent.

There was no dial tone.

Cursing, she pushed the buttons, hoping it would reset the phone. But it didn't. There was no static, nothing, just the sound of a phone that wasn't working.

"Stay calm," she mumbled to herself.

This could be some sort of weird outage around town, maybe from the equipment the television stations had brought in to cover the parade. Yes. That had to be it. Every year, at least a half dozen camera crews set up to film the governor on the parade float. That meant a lot of wireless signals that could possibly jam communication. In other words, there was a reasonable explanation.

But this didn't feel *reasonable.*

Bailey hung up the house phone and slipped her cell back into her pocket so her hands would be free. She still tried to keep calm, but nothing was working. Her breathing was way too fast, and she felt on the verge of a panic attack. She steadied herself by going to the front window and peeking out.

Nothing.

No one was there waiting to fire shots.

She looked at the end of the street. There were no floats going by yet. It would take a while for that to happen since Parker's neighborhood was on the last leg of the parade route, but she could see a few people who had gathered at the end of the block. They weren't exactly in shouting distance and their backs were to her, but then she had no reason to shout.

Little by little, Bailey leveled her breathing and tried to focus her thoughts on Zach and Parker. They needed all the positive vibes they could get right now, and since she might not get an update anytime soon, she just had to wait this out. It wouldn't do Zach or Parker any good if she turned into a basket case.

She looked again at the parade route and saw something.

A man.

He wasn't with the others at the end of the street. The man was walking up the sidewalk toward Parker's house. And he wasn't just walking. He was hurrying, practically running, and he kept looking over his shoulder.

Bailey automatically stepped back so that he wouldn't be able to see her from the window, but she continued to watch.

It was Sidney Burrell.

That evaporated what little calmness she'd managed to regain. What was he doing here? Better yet, what did he want?

It was too much to hope that he was visiting someone in the neighborhood. Besides, there probably wasn't a single person but her in any of the houses. Everyone was at the parade.

Bailey tried her phone again. Still no service. And she tightened her grip on the handle of the gun.

"Please don't come closer," she whispered.

But that's exactly what he did. Sidney looked over his shoulder again and started across the front lawn. Bailey lifted the gun, still praying that she didn't have to use it.

Then, Sidney stopped.

Another glance over his shoulder and down the street where the other people were standing. He said something that Bailey couldn't hear or understand, and he looked at the window where she was standing.

Bailey gasped and jumped back even farther, banging into a chair which, in turn, rammed into the coffee table. The pile of books toppled to the floor. The noise distracted her for just a second, and when her attention went back to the window, she saw Sidney running.

Oh, God.

He was running toward the house. Bailey stepped back even more and took aim at the front door. But Sidney didn't come onto the porch. Instead, he headed in the direction of the backyard.

Bailey turned to hurry toward the kitchen door, in case he tried to break in there, but she saw something else that stopped her in her tracks.

Another man.

It was Tim.

He had his gun drawn and was running after Sidney.

Her breath rattled in her chest, and Bailey raced to the kitchen. There was no sign of Sidney or Tim.

Where had they gone?

Bailey moved closer to the window but tried to keep some distance between her and the glass. She still couldn't see the men, but she heard something. Something or someone bashed against the side of the house, just on the other side of the wall. There were windows, but she didn't go closer to them.

She tried the house phone again. Still dead. Her cell phone wasn't working yet, either. So, all she could do was stand there, wait and pray.

Bailey didn't have to wait long.

There was another sound, as if someone had rammed into the wall again. And then she caught the movement from the corner of her eye.

Tim.

He staggered onto the back porch.

He had his hand clutched to his chest, and the front of his white shirt was soaked in blood.

PARKER RAN AS FAST AS HIS BODY would allow, but even that wasn't nearly fast enough. He wished he could fly over the logjam of people on Main Street.

"Move!" he shouted.

Some got out of his way, but most probably didn't even hear him. The high-school band was marching by, and the music was almost deafening. His shouts blended with the cheers and other sounds of people having fun.

Parker pushed his way through the crowd. He was half-crazy now with fear, and the only thing he could think of was getting to Zach so he could save him. His boy needed surgery, the nurse had said. Papers had to be signed before that could happen.

He broke through the line of people and nearly ran headfirst into a float. It was creeping along, and Parker had to wind his way around the back of it to cross to the other side. The crowd was still just as thick there, but he had to get through so he could reach the end of Main Street.

Each step was a challenge, like walking through mud with lead boots. He shouted again for people to move, but it did no good. The only thing he could do was keep trying because every inch was a victory. Soon, he'd be at the sheriff's office and afterward on the way to the hospital. Then, he would have more details.

The first question he would ask was about Zach's

condition. Whatever the answer, there had to be a solution. Parker was ready to sign the damn papers, donate blood, whatever it took, so that his son would live. Then, when he was sure Zach was out of danger, he needed to call Bailey and find out if his replacement had arrived.

"Bailey," he mumbled.

She had to be scared out of her mind, too, and Parker wished there had been a way for him to bring her with him. But after being sardined in this crowd, he was glad she was safe at his house.

Safe.

The word went through his head like a bullet that had been fired. His job was to keep Bailey safe and what were the odds that while he was trying to do just that, his son would be involved in an accident that would leave him in critical condition?

Parker shook his head.

Zach and he either had the worst luck on earth, or else...

That *or else* went through his head.

It was unthinkable, but Parker had to consider it at least. He took out his phone, not that he could hear anything, but he continued to make his way through the people as he hit the button to call Zach's cell.

Parker heard the phone ring. Barely. Heard it ring a second time, as well.

Then, someone answered.

For just a split second Parker thought it might be someone from the hospital or maybe one of the emergency responders to the accident.

But it wasn't.

"Dad?" he heard Zach say.

Parker froze. He couldn't believe he was hearing his son's voice. Was this some kind of trick his mind was playing on him? "Zach? Is that you?"

"Dad, if that's you, I can't hear you. Sounds like you're right in the middle of the parade."

"Son, are you all right?" Parker shouted. "Where are you?"

"I'm okay. I'm in front of the sheriff's office, where you said I could watch. I haven't left, I promise. What's wrong, Dad? Why do you sound so funny?"

Oh, hell. This couldn't be happening. But it was. Part of him was relieved to the bone that his son was all right, that he hadn't been in an accident. However, another part of him knew this spelled trouble.

For Bailey.

"Just stay where you are!" Parker switched directions and started to run. He prayed he wasn't too late to save her.

Chapter Fifteen

Bailey watched in horror as Tim staggered across the back porch.

Oh, mercy.

Even though she hadn't heard a shot, it certainly looked as if that's what had happened. Or maybe he'd been stabbed.

Either way, something bad had happened to him.

She could only guess that Sidney had been the one who had attacked Tim. But where was he? Was he still out there waiting to strike?

She could see Tim clearly through the window. He had his phone in his left hand. His gun, in his right. His face was covered with sweat, and there was all that blood on the front of his shirt.

He reached out to her. Their gazes connect for just a second.

And then he collapsed on the porch.

Bailey gasped and forced herself to move. Was he dead? She leaned closer to the window and saw that Tim was still moving.

She knew that opening the door was a huge risk, but

it was one she had to take. She couldn't stand there and let Tim bleed to death. Maybe, just maybe, his phone had service so that she could call for help. It would take ages for an emergency vehicle to get through the parade, but she had to try.

Bailey kept a grip on the gun she'd taken from Parker's cabinet, and she disengaged the security system so she could ease open the door. She braced herself for Sidney to jump out at her. This could be exactly what he wanted her to do so he could take his revenge for her firing him.

With a death grip on her gun, she hesitated in the doorway and glanced all around the yard. To the trees. The shrubs. Even the greenbelt where Parker had left minutes earlier.

No sign of Sidney.

Maybe he'd run after he had shot Tim.

Tim was facedown on the porch, just inches away. He groaned and lifted his head slightly. It was risky to move him since it could worsen his injuries, but there wasn't a choice. They couldn't stay on the back porch because Sidney might return and kill them both.

Bailey caught onto Tim's shoulder, turned him on his back and pulled hard on his arm. It didn't work. He was a lot heavier than she was, and she couldn't make him budge. Rather than spend another second out in the open, she slid her gun inside the house and onto the floor so she could use both hands to maneuver the dead weight.

Finally, she got him in.

But *in* wasn't good enough. Bailey had to drag Tim

across the kitchen, deep enough into the room so she could shut the door and lock it. Sidney Burrell was big and strong, and a locked door probably wouldn't hold him back if he truly wanted to get inside, but she didn't want to make this any easier for him.

Bailey took the time to punch in the code to rearm the security system. Even though the phones weren't working, maybe the system was still being monitored. If Sidney broke through that door, hopefully the security company would alert the sheriff.

"I have to use your phone," she said to Tim. He had it clutched in his left hand, and he was still moaning. He needed medical attention, and he needed it fast.

She dropped to her knees and wrenched the phone from him. Her stomach knotted when she looked on the screen and saw No Service.

Oh, God.

What now?

Bailey forced herself not to panic. Her first-aid skills were limited to bandaging scraped knees and minor cuts from accidents on the Cradles to Crayons' playground. This wasn't minor. There was way too much blood for that.

Dreading what she might see, she caught onto the sides of Tim's shirt and ripped it open. The buttons flew in the air, pinging against the tiled floor when they landed around Bailey and him.

There was some blood on his chest, not nearly as much though as she'd expected, but it was more than enough to require Bailey to take a deep breath before she could continue. What she couldn't see was the point of entry for the bullet, and she needed to find it so she could apply some pressure and stop the bleeding.

"Where did Sidney shoot you?" she asked, turning him slightly on his side so she could examine him.

"He didn't," Tim answered.

Bailey's gaze whipped in the direction of his face, but it was already too late. Tim came off the floor, dragging her up with him.

And he put the gun to her head. "Now we can have some fun," he growled.

PARKER COULDN'T PRESS IN Bailey's phone number fast enough. He had to warn her and warn her *now* that she was in danger. But her phone didn't ring. Instead, he heard the recorded message.

Service is temporarily unavailable.

What the hell did that mean?

Parker cursed and tried his home phone. It wasn't an identical message, but it was close. Something was definitely wrong, maybe the lines had even been jammed, because that phone had worked less than fifteen minutes ago.

He considered calling the sheriff next, but he was wasting precious time. So, he ran, fighting his way back through the crowd.

While he ran, Parker said a prayer of thanks for his son's safety, but he also cursed himself.

He should have seen this coming.

Bailey's stalker had been relentless, and whoever he was, he must have known that the Fourth of July was the perfect day to strike. The sheriff and deputies were tied up with the parade. The streets were closed, making it difficult for the authorities to respond to a 9-1-1- call. And now the SOB had managed to get Bailey's bodyguard out of the house.

That call about Zach being in an accident had done the trick.

The stalker had probably paid someone to make the call. Hell, the guy might have been watching the house when Parker went running outside to get to the hospital. He could have already broken in by now.

Parker ran faster, so fast that it felt as if his heart might burst in his chest.

He reminded himself that Bailey had a gun. Or at least he hoped she'd had time to get it out of the locked cabinet before all hell had broken loose. Maybe she'd even had time to call the sheriff before the phones had stopped working. She certainly hadn't called him, and Parker was actually hoping the non-service for the phones was the reason she hadn't communicated with him.

Of course, he also had to consider the possibility that the stalker had incapacitated her in some way.

His blood turned cold, and the acid rose in his throat.

Parker couldn't bear the thought of someone hurting Bailey. Or worse. He could lose her and all because he'd been stupid enough to fall for a crank call.

He battled his way through the last part of the crowd and raced to the greenbelt. Parker drew his gun and mentally prepared himself for the fight.

The trees and branches in the greenbelt were heavy

with foliage. Parker hoped that would help conceal him in case the stalker was watching for his return. He raced behind the massive live oaks, using them for cover until he made it to his backyard.

He glanced around. This was the same spot the gunman had used to set up that remote-control gun, and he could see the kitchen windows while still maintaining cover.

What he couldn't see was Bailey.

The door was closed, maybe a good sign. Maybe the stalker hadn't struck yet. Or maybe he was inside. Parker had to get closer so he could find out.

He kept his gun ready and ran to the back porch. He braced himself for gunfire but there was nothing. Just silence.

And then he saw the blood.

There. On the white-painted porch floor, there were drops of blood. But whose? He nearly lost his breath thinking that it might be Bailey's.

The rage and pain boiled up inside, and Parker had to fight his primal instincts to bash down the door. He couldn't give in to the emotion. There was a chance that he could use the element of surprise and sneak up on this guy. After all, the stalker thought Parker was on the way to the hospital, and he might believe he had more time.

Time with Bailey.

That required a deep breath, and Parker hurried to the other side of the porch so he could look in the window from a different angle. He saw more blood.

Lots of it.

Parker choked back a groan and followed the trail, praying that he wouldn't find Bailey's body at the end of it.

It didn't take him long to realize that something was definitely wrong. He wasn't a blood-spatter expert, but the drops didn't appear to be in the right pattern for someone bleeding out. No. It was as if someone had dribbled the blood on the porch.

But why?

Had the stalker done that to scare Bailey? Was this just another act of vandalism? Parker wanted to believe that, but everything in his gut told him otherwise.

Whatever was going on, it was bad.

Parker continued to follow the blood, but he kept watch at the window. He listened too for any sound that would give him a clue as to what was going on.

He soon got that clue.

When he reached the edge of the house, he saw the body. The sickening dread clawed away at him, and he made himself look closer.

It wasn't Bailey.

Thank God.

The body was male. It was Sidney Burrell, and from the looks of him, he'd been shot at point-blank range in the chest.

Parker swallowed hard. Had Bailey heard the shot and come out? Maybe she was hiding inside. He had to hold on to that hope because the alternative wasn't something he could handle right now.

He stepped onto the porch, trying not to make a sound, and he looked into the kitchen. Parker didn't see anyone, and there was no sign of a struggle. His cup of coffee was still sitting undisturbed on the counter.

Maybe his gut was wrong.

If so, if Bailey was safe and sound, then Parker intended to pull her in his arms, kiss her and tell her exactly how much he cared for her.

He moved past the window, heading toward the door. But the shadow caught his eye. He looked harder and rethought that. It wasn't a shadow. There was a person in between the kitchen and the small laundry room.

"Bailey?" he softly called out.

He waited, hoping that she would answer. But she didn't. However, there was some movement.

Parker moved closer to the window and saw someone. Not Bailey. It was a man, and he was stripping off his shirt. His back was to Parker so he couldn't see the man's face. It could be Chester Herman or Tim. Hell, it could be a total stranger. But Parker did see something else.

The gun in the man's hand.

And the blood on his stark white shirt.

That jacked up his heart rate.

Where was Bailey? Had this SOB done something to her?

Parker started to bolt toward the back door so he could kick it in, but he stopped when the man finally moved. The guy stepped back just a few inches into the kitchen.

Just enough for Parker to see Bailey.

She was against the laundry-room wall. She was alive, thank God. Parker couldn't see any injuries, and she was glaring at the man who was now in the process of putting on one of Parker's black T-shirts.

Parker didn't care why he was doing that. He only wanted to get Bailey safely out of there.

But how?

Was this man planning to take her somewhere? Was that why he'd changed from his blood-stained shirt? Parker was betting the blood wasn't his. It probably belonged to the now-dead Sidney Burrell.

Bailey's glare got worse, and she looked ready to launch herself at the man. Since her captor was armed, Parker didn't want her to do that. No. He needed to get into the house and put an end to this.

Parker took one last look at the situation so he could assess the best way to get inside. But he also kept Bailey in his line of sight. That's how he was able to see the change in her expression. Her glare softened. Her eyes widened.

She'd seen him.

Parker knew instantly that was a mistake, and he got his gun ready. He didn't have time to adjust his aim.

The man turned and fired a shot directly at Parker.

Chapter Sixteen

Bailey screamed for Parker to get down, but it was too late.

Tim turned, aiming the gun he'd rigged with a silencer, and the bullet blasted through the window. Glass flew everywhere, and Parker disappeared from sight. Bailey didn't know if he'd been shot or if he'd managed to get away in time.

Bailey launched herself at him. She didn't have a weapon. Tim had kicked her gun into the hall. But she did have her hands and body. And she also had the rage that she let fuel her attack. She was not going to stand by and let Tim get off another shot at Parker.

She didn't recognize the sound that came from her mouth, but it obviously alerted Tim. He swung back around, but before he could aim the gun again at her, Bailey put down her head and plowed right into him.

It was like hitting a wall.

He was solid and had obviously honed his body to be a lethal weapon. Even putting her entire weight into her launch, Bailey still didn't knock him to the floor.

Not good. She'd counted on a hard fall in the hopes she could dislodge the gun from his hand.

Tim called her a vile name and slammed her against the washing machine. She hit so hard that it knocked the breath out of her. Bailey couldn't move. She couldn't fight back. She could only stand there and gasp for air.

Even over the roaring in head, she heard the sound and realized that someone was bashing down the kitchen door.

Parker.

He was alive.

Bailey didn't have time to feel any relief about that because Tim latched onto her hair and dragged her in front of him. He jammed the gun right against her temple, just as the door gave way.

Parker burst through the opening. His gun was ready and aimed. But so was Tim's. And she could see in Parker's eyes that he realized she was Tim's hostage and his human shield.

"Zach?" she said.

"He's fine. There was no accident."

Despite the awful circumstances, Bailey was so glad that nothing had happened to Parker's son.

"I figure Tim hired someone to make that call," Parker explained. His voice was so calm, but every muscle in his body was tensed to the point of looking painful. He kept his gun aimed, but he didn't come closer. He stayed put, with this attention fastened to Tim.

"I did hire someone," Tim readily admitted. "A former acquaintance who owed me a favor."

"This acquaintance could have already gone to the sheriff," Parker pointed out.

"Probably not. She's an addict and tends to avoid the cops. But she was rather good sneaking into the nurse's lounge at the E.R. to use their phone. And since I used a jammer to stop Bailey from calling, I can only guess that no one is on the way here to provide backup."

"Don't bet on that," Parker snarled. "My phone wasn't jammed when I realized this was a ruse and that Bailey was in danger. I called the sheriff, and he's on his way here."

She couldn't see Tim's expression, but Bailey thought he might have smiled. "Bravo, Captain McKenna. I figured with your combat instincts, you wouldn't waste precious time to request backup. After all, your ego is so big that you probably thought you could handle me all by yourself."

"I can," Parker assured him.

Bailey believed that. If this were a fair fight. But it wasn't. Tim had her as his shield, and that meant Parker wouldn't fire a shot because she could be hit.

"Neither Sheriff Hale nor I can let you just walk out of here," Parker warned. He took a small step closer. "You murdered Sidney Burrell."

Oh, God. So, that's what had happened. That's why Tim had blood on his shirt.

"Sidney was a casualty of war," Tim said, the smugness oozing through each word. "He was innocent, you know. Well, innocent of stalking Bailey anyway."

"What about Chester Herman?" Parker made another step.

"Only slightly involved. I did hire him to drive around and toss out that note, but everything else, I did."

"Why?" Bailey demanded.

"Why?" He jammed the gun even harder against her temple. So hard that Bailey felt her skin bruise.

"Because you're mine, that's why. You were just too stupid to realize that. Instead, you climbed into bed with this jarhead."

"I've never been yours," she countered despite the pain.

"Wrong. You would have eventually seen the light, if your so-called bodyguard hadn't come into the picture."

"How do you figure that?" Parker asked. Another step.

Tim jammed the gun even harder. "Move another inch, and I'll kill her right here where she stands."

Parker stopped, but his rage was so strong that it was palatable.

"I was supposed to save her," Tim growled.

Parker blinked. "Excuse me?"

"Save her!" Tim practically yelled. "I wanted Bailey to think she was in danger. That's why I sent the notes. That's why I slashed her tires and trashed her office. That's why I rigged that gun to fire shots at your house."

"You thought doing those things would *save* her?" Parker demanded.

"No!" Tim's tone made it sound as if the answer were obvious and that Parker and she were idiots for not understanding this *plan* he had. "Those things were only meant to scare her. To make her think she was in danger. I was going to seal all the windows and doors in her house and then set fire to it."

Parker's jaw muscles turned to iron. "You were going to do what?"

Bailey could only manage an "Oh, God." A crazy man had Parker and her at gunpoint.

"I wouldn't have let her burn," Tim said, apparently disgusted that Parker had assumed that. "I would have broken down the door and saved her. I knew that would be the tipping point. Women can't resist a hero. She would have ended up in my arms. And in my bed. That ring I bought for her—that would have become her engagement ring."

She nearly gagged. It was a risk to antagonize him, but Bailey couldn't help herself. "You're not a hero. You're a disgusting egotistical lunatic. You risked Parker and Zach's lives so you could have me. Well, guess what? You can never have me. *Never.*"

Tim still had hold of her hair with his left hand, and he snapped back her head. "We'll see about that. Back up, soldier boy," he ordered Parker.

"Why? What do you think you're going to do?" Parker ordered right back. "Because I'm not letting you escape."

"You don't have a say in the matter. The only reason I don't intend to kill you right now is because I want you to have to live with the fact that I'll have Bailey and you won't."

"What do you mean?" Bailey asked.

"I mean, you will be mine. That never doesn't apply.

Because this isn't your decision to make. It's mine, and I've already made it."

He was going to take her by force. But take her where? Bailey didn't want to think about that. She only wanted to deal with this moment. Somehow, she had to get away from Tim so that Parker would have a clean shot.

Tim used his body to nudge Bailey forward. "I said back up," he told Parker again. "And if you try to stop me, I'll forgo that little pleasure of having you live with losing Bailey. I'll splatter parts of you all over this kitchen. Think of your son," Tim added, his tone now sappy sweet and totally insincere.

Bailey had to rein in her temper. As much as she wanted to hurt Tim, she couldn't risk that. She knew without a doubt that he would indeed kill Parker. And she couldn't live with herself if that happened.

Tim gave Bailey another jab with his gun. Parker cursed and backed up. What he didn't do was lower his weapon. He kept it trained right on them. Good. She wanted him ready.

"Where are you taking me?" Bailey demanded.

"To a new life." Tim shoved her forward, and Parker stepped back, giving Tim enough room to reach the gaping hole where the door had once been.

"I prefer the life I have now." She locked gazes with Parker, hoping that he would give her some kind of signal as to how they could prevent Tim from getting her outside.

"That's because you have no idea how good things

can be with me," Tim answered. "I can make you happy, Bailey. You'll see."

She kept her weight pressing back against him so it would be harder for Tim to force her to move. It slowed him down a little, but he still made it to the doorway.

"I have a car waiting to take you to a new life. But here's the catch. I had to park on the other side of Main Street. That means we have to cut through the parade crowd."

Bailey shook her head. "People will see us. They'll see your gun." Someone could be hurt if they tried to stop Tim, and someone would. The entire town wouldn't just stand by and wait for the right moment to put an end to this.

"I got a plan for that, too. Once we're on Main, I'll put the gun in my pocket, but it'll be aimed right at your spine. A bullet to the head isn't the only way to kill someone. Remember that when we're walking. Cooperate and everyone lives."

Parker's eyes narrowed to slits. "You know I'm coming after you."

"Yes, I expected as much. But you won't do anything as long as I have a gun on Bailey. And she won't do anything, either." He gave her a jab with the gun. "Because if anything goes wrong, I'll start shooting, and I'll kill as many people as I can."

The fear sliced through her. Not for her life. No. The stakes were much higher than that. Her family and Zach were at that parade. Her friends, too. There'd be other families, children. Innocent people who had done nothing to be in this lunatic's path.

Bailey figured if anyone died today, it would be her.

"Let's go," Tim snarled, and with the gun barrel grinding into her head, he pushed her out onto the porch. "See you later, solider boy."

Tim turned, keeping her in front of him, and with her in tow, he started toward the greenbelt.

PARKER DIDN'T TAKE HIS EYES off Tim's trigger finger.

It was a challenge because the last time he'd gotten a glimpse of Bailey's face, Parker had seen the fear. The anger. And then the resignation. She wouldn't let Tim start shooting.

She would sacrifice herself.

Parker had no plans to let her do that.

Tim continued to walk backward to the greenbelt. Parker followed, waiting for the right time. He bracketed his right wrist so he'd have a steadier shot if the opportunity arose. So far, Tim had played it perfectly. He'd ducked down enough that Parker didn't have a head shot, and that was the only kind of shot that he was certain would take out the man before Tim could pull the trigger.

It took every ounce of Parker's willpower and training to stop himself from charging this SOB and beating him to a bloody pulp. Tim had endangered his son and now Bailey. And Parker was not going to let him get away with any of it. Tim would pay, and he would pay hard.

Parker didn't try to reason with the man. He knew he would be wasting his breath. Tim obviously had a plan that included a vehicle parked somewhere. He probably had made other travel arrangements. Maybe Tim thought he could get Bailey to somewhere like Mexico where he could brainwash her into loving him. And when the brainwashing didn't work, and it wouldn't, then he would kill her.

Tim slowed when Bailey and he reached the thick underbrush in the greenbelt, and he continued to glance over his shoulder. There was no pattern to the glances. No way to predict them. But that's what Bailey seemed to be doing. She kept glancing back, too, and Parker hoped like the devil that she didn't do anything rash, because Tim wouldn't miss a point-blank range shot.

Neither would Parker.

But he wasn't sure when he'd get one.

He hated the idea of Tim making his way through the parade-goers, but Parker might have to let that happen. His best chance might be when Tim made it to the vehicle. Tim would have to get Bailey inside and into the seat, and during that process he wouldn't be able to use her to shield his body.

That's when Parker would have to kill him.

Since Parker wasn't a killer by nature, he would have liked to have the chance to talk Tim into surrendering. Then, he could be hauled off to jail. But Tim wasn't the surrendering type.

No.

This would end with somebody dead. And it wasn't going to be Bailey.

Tim came out of the greenbelt and got onto the sidewalk that led to Main Street. So did Parker, and he kept about seven yards' distance between them. Just ahead, he could see a few people watching a float that was creeping past them. No one was looking back at the felony in progress.

When Tim got closer to the people and the parade, he did as he said. He slipped his gun into his pocket, keeping it pressed against Bailey. What he didn't do was take his eyes off Parker. He kept watch to make sure Parker wasn't about to dive at him.

Parker didn't put his gun in his pocket, but he did lower it to his side. He hoped it was enough. He didn't want people to see it and then panic. That could cause Tim to start firing.

The sounds of the people and music were suddenly all around them. So many possible distractions, so many things that could go wrong. But Parker didn't look away from Tim.

Tim smiled again. It was as slick and oily as he was. And he moved nearly back-to-back with an elderly woman who was waving at someone on the float. The woman didn't see what was coming.

Parker did.

But he couldn't stop it.

Tim latched onto the woman and shoved her right at Parker. She screamed, but she couldn't stop the movement from Tim's fierce push. She flew into Parker. He kept his balance and somehow grabbed onto her so that she wouldn't fall.

The whole thing took just a few seconds. But during those precious seconds, Parker had no choice but to take his gaze off Tim. When he looked up again, Tim and Bailey had melted into the crowd of people.

Hell.

"Get down!" Parker shouted to those in front of him. Some heard him. Most didn't. Most looked around as if trying to figure out what was going on.

What was going on was that Tim was trying to get away.

Parker elbowed his way through the parade-goers and tried to get sight of Tim. His heart jumped to his throat when he didn't see them, but he continued to look.

There.

He spotted Bailey's red dress.

Tim had her on the other side of the street, which meant he'd managed to dart in between the floats. Bailey was frantically looking around, for Parker no doubt, but the rest of the crowd seemed oblivious to what was going on.

Parker fastened his attention on Bailey. He didn't want to lose her again in the crowd, and he began to make his way up the sidewalk. He had to get around a group of jugglers who were performing between the floats. He finally got a break and tore through the performers.

But Tim was already on the move.

He had a death grip on Bailey and was using her to plow his way through the crowd. Some people complained about Tim's shoving and pushing, but no one was stopping him. Probably because they hadn't seen the gun that Tim had pointed at Bailey's spine.

"Dad!" Parker heard Zach call out.

His heart went to his knees, and he fired glances all around the crowd until he spotted his son. Hell. Zach was only a few yards in front of Tim and Bailey. Zach would soon see them, and he would know something was wrong. He would try to help, and that could get him hurt. Tim's gun was rigged with a silencer so he could shoot Zach and no one in the crowd would even hear it.

"Move!" Parker shouted to Zach.

But Zach shook his head and put his fingers to his ear. His son couldn't hear him. But Parker could see what was about to happen. It was like watching a train wreck.

Parker tried, but he had to fight for every inch of ground. He watched as Tim pushed through the people between Zach and him, and he knew the exact moment that Tim had seen his son.

Bailey saw Zach, too, and she began to struggle. She wasn't trying to get away, Parker realized. She was trying to put herself between Zach and Tim.

She was trying to save his son.

Zach's face said it all. He had no idea what was going on, but he knew Bailey was in some kind of trouble. He moved forward, even though Bailey yelled for him to stay back.

People stepped in and out of Parker's view so he could only get glimpses of what was going on. He couldn't breathe. He couldn't let himself think beyond this split second of saving Zach and Bailey.

Parker broke through the crowd and to the other side. But it was already too late. Tim's smile told him that.

"Do you really want your son to witness your death, or Bailey's?" Tim asked. He volleyed glances between Bailey and Parker.

Thankfully, Zach didn't move. Maybe because he

was frozen with fear. His eyes were wide, and he stared at Parker, obviously waiting for his dad to save Bailey and him.

But Parker couldn't do anything, not with the risk that Tim might shoot Bailey or him in front of Zach. Tim was right about one thing—Parker didn't want his son to witness that.

"Come on," Tim said, the smile curving his mouth again. "Zach can play this game, too. Maybe this will *encourage* both of you to cooperate. Because one way or another, Bailey is leaving with me."

BAILEY WANTED TO SCREAM AND tear Tim limb from limb. It was bad enough that Tim was trying to control her like a puppet, but now he'd involved Zach in this lethal scheme to possess her and make her love him.

"I'm so sorry," she mouthed to Zach.

Zach just shook his head, obviously not understanding, but his gaze did drop to Tim's pocket, where Zach probably noticed the gun.

"Hi, Bailey!" someone called out. It was Faith, the owner of the diner. She was on the other side of the street and was smiling.

Bailey waved back and tried to return the smile. Faith was pregnant, and while Bailey would have liked someone to be alerted, she didn't want Faith and her unborn baby in the middle of this mix. Bailey turned away from her so the woman hopefully wouldn't see that anything was wrong.

"Don't move, Zach," Parker told him, and his gaze

snapped to Tim. "If you hurt either of them, you're a dead man."

"I believe I'm the one controlling the shots here," Tim snapped. "Let's go. We're all going to take a little trip to the car now." He glanced around, probably to see if anyone was paying attention.

There didn't appear to be, but then most people were watching the approach of the next float. When someone did make eye contact with Tim, he just smiled as if nothing was wrong. Bailey tried to do the same.

Tim started to move, shoving Bailey and latching onto Zach's arm to force the boy to go with him. Parker followed. Each step was agony, and Bailey prayed that they could all make it out of this safely. Zach couldn't lose his father, and Parker couldn't lose Zach.

She had to do something.

"Please," she said to Tim. She tried to use a civil tone and also forced her expression to soften. It was a mask, all right, because Bailey hated this man with every fiber of her being. "Don't do this. I'll go with you voluntarily. Just let Zach and Parker go."

Tim ducked into an open wrought-iron gate that led to the city park. It was less crowded here, but there were still a few people milling around, including a woman who was trying to soothe a crying baby. Tim kept his gun low but still aimed at Zach.

"I'm sorry," Zach immediately said to Parker. "When you called, you sounded so funny, so I thought I'd go to the house and check on you."

Parker shook his head. "It's all right. You didn't do anything wrong."

"Touching," Tim snarled, and he looked at Bailey. "You'd actually give up yourself for his kid?" he asked, sounding confused.

Bailey already knew the answer so she didn't have to give it any thought. "In a heartbeat. There's no need to do this, Tim. I'll go with you. I'll do anything you want me to do. Just let him go. Keep the gun aimed at me, and we'll walk away from here."

Tim stared at her several long moments and then cursed. "You're in love with McKenna."

She was about to deny it, but Bailey was afraid the denial would stick in her throat. What a time to realize her true feelings, but she knew it was true.

She was indeed in love with Parker.

Bailey swallowed hard. "Let's just go to the car. You and me. We leave them here, and they'll stay because Parker doesn't want his son in danger any more than I do." She aimed a warning glance at Parker to make sure he understood.

But it didn't stay a glance.

Their gazes connected. And held. She could see that this was ripping him to pieces. Parker was no doubt reliving every horrible moment of his wife and unborn child's deaths. He was thinking déjà vu, and it was killing him.

"Stay here," she insisted. "Get Zach to safety. I'll be all right."

But she had zero intentions of getting into a vehicle with Tim. No. Once he realized he couldn't force her to love him, then he would kill her. But first, he would make her life a living hell.

That wasn't going to happen.

When Parker had Zach safely away, she would attack Tim. She didn't have his strength or training. She didn't have a gun. But Bailey had something that Tim didn't: the will to escape. Even if she died in that fight, it would be an easier way to go than what he had in mind for her.

"Goodbye," she said first to Zach and then she repeated it to Parker. She narrowed her eyes, hoping he would do as she wanted. He didn't give her confirmation of that, and she didn't wait for one.

"Let's go," she told Tim.

She could see the debate in Tim's eyes. Parker and Zach were also trying to figure a way out of this. But Tim finally nodded and moved toward her.

Bailey turned, but from the corner of her eye, she saw Parker move, too. Tim didn't miss what was happening. He brought up his gun, to aim it at Zach.

"Get down!" Bailey yelled to Zach. But she was terrified that he wouldn't be able to do that.

Bailey dove at Zach, throwing her entire weight against him. Everything suddenly seemed to happen in slow motion, even the sound of her voice as she continued to yell for Zach to move out of the way.

She plowed into Zach, knocking them both to the ground, but Bailey didn't stay there. She whirled around so she could get up and go after Tim.

But she was too late.

Bailey could only watch as Tim aimed his gun. Not at Zach or Parker, thank God.

But at her.

Tim was going to shoot her.

He pulled the trigger. More slow motion. The swishing sound was drowned out by a blast thick and loud. So loud that it cut through the noise of the parade.

Someone screamed. Maybe it was her. Bailey couldn't be sure.

Because the world closed in around her.

Chapter Seventeen

Parker hadn't wanted to pull the trigger. Not in front of Bailey and his son.

But Tim gave him no choice.

When Tim took aim at Bailey, Parker had seen the look in his eyes. This was it. Tim wouldn't back down. He was going to kill her.

So, Parker fired, praying that he got off his shot before Tim did.

And Parker didn't miss.

The bullet slammed into Tim's chest causing his body and his shooting arm to jerk back. Tim stood there for several long seconds, a frozen look on his face. Then, he crumpled to the ground in a dead heap.

"Oh, God," he heard Bailey say.

Parker whipped his gaze in her direction, praying that neither Zach nor she had been hurt, but there were no signs of blood or injury. Thank God. Tim had gotten off a shot, Parker was sure of that, but he hoped it had gone into the ground or the fence.

He went closer, frantically looking, trying to make sure they were indeed all right. There wasn't a drop of color in Bailey's face. She was in front of Zach, her body between Tim's and his. She reached back, latched onto Zach and pulled him against her shoulder so that he wouldn't see the body.

Even now, she was still protecting his son.

"Are you okay?" Parker asked both of them.

Zach managed a nod.

"You're alive," Bailey mouthed. The tears sprang to her eyes, but Parker was pretty sure they were tears of relief. There was no time to tell her that he was relieved, too.

People began to shout. The shot he'd fired into Tim had no doubt drawn their attention. Someone was yelling for the sheriff. Good. The sooner Sheriff Hale arrived, the sooner they could move the body out of there. The parade would be ruined for anyone who saw or heard about the shooting, but it was far better than the alternative.

He could have lost Bailey and Zach.

"Could you get Zach out of here?" he asked Bailey and hoped she had the energy left to do that.

She gave him a shaky nod. She was shaking, too, but Bailey somehow got to her feet, and with Zach pressed against her, she led him out of the park and onto the other side of the fence.

Parker went closer to Tim to verify that he was dead. He didn't need the verification, but he did it anyway. Old habits. He looked down at the man who had made Bailey's life hell, and he cursed. What a waste. Murder and attempted murder, all in the name of love.

Parker knew what love was, and that wasn't it.

"You okay?" Sheriff Hale shouted as he came tearing through the gate. He had his gun drawn, and he wasn't alone. One of the deputies was right behind him.

"Yeah." But he was sure he would see Tim in his nightmares. It had taken ten years off Parker's life when Tim had pointed that gun at Bailey.

"He was going to kill her," Parker explained. "Tim was the stalker."

Sheriff Hale cursed and stared down at the body. "Didn't see that one coming."

No one had. Especially not Bailey, or she wouldn't have let the man into the house. To Tim's credit though, he'd been damn good at tricking them.

The deputy pulled out his phone and began to make the necessary calls.

"I'll tell the governor," Sheriff Hale said. He glanced around. "And I'll close off this area so none of the kids see this."

"Bring in Chester Herman, too," Parker suggested. "Tim confessed to hiring him. He also paid a woman to make a bogus call from the hospital." Though those were minor compared to what Tim had done.

"Will do," the sheriff promised.

Someone came rushing through the gate. It was Deputy Bracken, Josh's dad. He looked at the body and then at Parker. "I'm so sorry, Parker. Zach just told me what happened. I can't believe Zach got out of my sight that way. One minute he was there, and the next minute, he wasn't. Hell. He said Tim had a gun."

"He did. But it's all right," Parker assured him. "Everyone is safe now."

Deputy Bracken shook his head and cursed again. “Everyone except for Bailey.”

Everything inside Parker went still. “What do you mean?”

The deputy just stared at him as if Parker had lost his mind. “Didn’t you know?”

“Know what?” Parker latched onto the deputy’s shirt.

“Bailey’s on the way to the hospital,” the deputy told him. “She was shot.”

BAILEY WAS ABOUT TO LOSE IT.

“It’s a scratch,” she told the medic for the umpteenth time.

But he kept on dabbing at it with disinfectant that stung like fire. She was grateful that the wound wasn’t more serious—it easily could have been—but this kind of attention should be reserved for patients in critical condition and not someone with a bullet graze on her arm.

Bailey was about to move the medic aside and leave, but then she heard a familiar voice. It was Parker. And he was shouting her name.

She got off the examining table in the E.R. and hurried to the doorway. Parker was manhandling a medic and demanding to know where she was.

“I’m here,” she called out.

He snapped toward her, looked her over from head to toe. He was what her Granny Lockhart would have called a sight for sore eyes, and Bailey wondered if there would be a time when Parker could walk into a room and not take her breath away.

She hoped not.

Bailey smiled. A smile he didn't return, and for a moment she had a horrible thought. "Is Zach okay?"

"He's fine." His hand was shaking when he motioned behind him, and she saw Zach, the sheriff and her mother.

They all came rushing toward her, but Parker got there first. He looked at her arm.

"It's a scratch," she stated.

He'd obviously expected something much worse because his breath swooshed out, and he pulled her to him. The hug was hard, long and very welcome.

"Deputy Bracken said you'd been shot," Parker mumbled.

"Technically, I was. But it's a scratch."

"You were shot." His voice was practically soundless. "You could have been killed."

"But I wasn't." She pulled away from him so she could make eye contact with him.

The others—her mother, Zach and the sheriff—all came closer. So did the medic she'd left in the examining room. He came out and proceeded to put a bandage on her arm.

"Are you sure you're okay?" Zach asked.

"Positive." She turned and showed him her arm just seconds before it was covered with the bandage which was little more than an adhesive strip. "Deputy Bracken overreacted. So did the nurse who was standing next to me when she saw the blood. She insisted I come to the hospital, and she and her husband practically shoved me into one of the emergency-response vehicles and drove me here."

Her mother was crying, and Parker stepped back so that Lila could pull Bailey into her arms. "It's okay, Mom. I promise."

"But Tim..." Her voice broke.

"Is no longer a threat," Bailey finished. "Thanks to Parker."

"Told you Dad was like a superhero," Zach said, adding a shrug while his hands were crammed into his jeans' pockets.

Thank God he didn't seem traumatized by the shooting, but he did move nearer to his dad. Parker slid his arm around the boy's shoulders, and Zach leaned into him.

"You're crying, Bailey," her mother announced, and Lila got tears in her eyes, too.

"Because of them." Bailey tipped her head to Parker and Zach. They were getting closer, and that would be good for both of them.

"Oh." Lila looked at father and son and then at Bailey. She blinked. "You're in love with Parker."

Bailey huffed. Tim had said that very same thing. What, was she wearing her heart on her sleeve or something?

She glanced at the others and saw they were all looking at her as if waiting for an answer.

Especially Parker.

Bailey considered putting this off, until Parker and

she were alone, but what the heck? Apparently, everyone knew anyway.

"Yes," she admitted to her mother. "I'm in love with him."

Lila squealed with delight, but Bailey ignored her and focused on Parker and Zach. It was their opinions that counted most, and she hoped she hadn't put Parker in an embarrassing place with her confession.

What had she done?

Parker wasn't moving, wasn't reacting. He was just staring at her.

She was ready to panic when she saw Zach smile. "Cool," he mumbled. "When your arm gets better, maybe we can shoot some hoops."

"Absolutely," she managed to say distractedly. "I'd love that." Zach had said the perfect thing to make her feel better. But Bailey was still holding her breath and waiting for Parker.

He finally stepped closer, and he looked at the others. "Uh, could you give Bailey and me a minute alone?"

Oh, God. He was going to dump her.

But then, Parker shook his head. "Wait," he told them. He looked at Zach. "This might work better if all of you are around."

Now, Parker looked at her, and the corner of his mouth lifted in that half smile that drove her crazy and made her hot all over. "She's in love with me," he said over his shoulder to all of them.

"Yes. I am." Bailey held her breath and waited.

"Good. Because I'm in love with you, too…."

He continued to talk, but Bailey didn't hear a word of

anything else. She only heard *I'm in love with you, too,* and that caused her to jump into his arms. She kissed him, pulled back and smiled so Parker could see how happy she was, and then kissed him again.

"You're not just saying that, right?" she clarified.

"I'm saying it because it's true." And he whispered it in her ear. "I love you, Bailey."

"Uh, I should probably go," the sheriff said. "Got things to do. Zach, um, you want me to drop you off at Josh Bracken's house?"

There was an implied *to give these lovebirds some time alone* at the end of that question.

"I'll take him," Lila volunteered. "I have my limo outside, and the driver is one of Bart's men."

"A limo?" Zach questioned, clearly impressed. "Can I go with her, Dad?"

"Sure." Parker nodded not once but twice. "But I want you to be the first to know that I'm about to ask Bailey to marry me."

Oh, mercy. That took her breath away again, and Bailey might have done something as stupid as a swoon if Parker hadn't caught onto her.

"Really?" Zach asked at the moment Lila said, "Ohhhhh."

Sheriff Hale mumbled something about this being way too personal for outsiders, and he hurried away. So did the medic who'd been waiting behind her.

"Really," Parker promised.

"Does that mean she'll, like, get to move in with us?" Zach asked.

"I hope so," Bailey mumbled. "Because when your dad asks me to marry him, I intend to say yes."

Parker made a sound of relief and kissed her until it wasn't relief she was feeling.

Zach grinned and issued another, "Cool. She's going to say yes."

Lila repeated the "cool" and slipped her arm around Zach's shoulder. "Come on. On the way to Josh's, we'll stop at one of the parade booths for ice cream. Maybe some cotton candy, too."

"Don't overdo it, Mom," Bailey told her.

Lila dismissed that with the wave of her perfectly manicured hand. "I've waited years for a grandchild, and I finally have one. I think a little overdoing is exactly how Zach and I will celebrate your engagement."

Zach started to walk away with Bailey's mother, but then he stopped and rushed back to hug first Bailey and then his dad. It was brief. But perfect. It only added to the already perfect moment in the making.

As soon as Zach stepped away, Parker pulled her back into his arms. "You meant that, right? You're really going to say yes?"

"Absolutely." It was strange, everything suddenly seemed crystal clear. Bailey knew exactly what she wanted, and what she wanted was standing directly in front of her. "I love you, Parker."

"Good." He nodded, smiled. Kissed her. And he dropped down on one knee. "So, here's the official proposal. Bailey Lockhart, will you marry me?"

She dropped to her knees as well and gave him her

answer while her mouth was still touching his. "In a heartbeat."

The next kiss was considerably longer, and the nurse who passed by them cleared her throat. "You can probably find a spare room down the hall," she mumbled.

"I have a better idea," Parker whispered to Bailey. He touched his finger to her bandaged arm. "Let me take you home. Then, I can very gently strip off all your clothes and very gently make love to you."

Now, it was perfect.

This was the way she wanted to remember this Fourth of July. Not Tim. Not any of the bad things he'd done. She wanted all future memories to be of Zach's smile when he'd heard she was going to be his stepmom. She wanted the memories of Parker making love to her. Of his sizzling half smile. Of the way he was looking at her now. Bailey wanted it all, and she reached out and took it.

"Come on," Parker drawled. He got to his feet and scooped her up in his arms. "It's time to go home."

Epilogue

A wedding.

Lila couldn't stop smiling. She had waited for this for nearly a decade, and now it was happening. Bailey was getting married, and there was a wedding to plan.

A future to plan, too.

Now that Bailey and she no longer had someone threatening them, Lila could concentrate first on the wedding and then on her decision about whether or not to run for president.

There were things that had to be worked out for both.

She sat at her desk and began to thumb through the bridal magazines that her assistant had just brought in with the mail. The mail could wait, for a few minutes anyway, but Lila wanted to get a peek at the magazines.

Tears sprang to her eyes when she saw the first picture of a model in a ballerina-style wedding dress. It was probably too froufrou for Bailey, but Lila was sure she could talk her into some lacy and traditional.

Bailey was going to be such a beautiful bride.

Thankfully, neither Parker nor Bailey wanted to wait. With Zach's complete approval, they would be married the end of the month. That didn't give Lila much time, but she was so pleased to see Bailey this happy that she didn't care. Besides, she could hire an entire team to put together the perfect ceremony. The trick would be to pull it all off without making it a media circus.

This was a family occasion, and Lila didn't want anyone saying she was using it as publicity for her possible presidential candidacy.

She finished one of the magazines and thumbed through another. So many possibilities. Maybe Bailey would even consider wearing Lila's own wedding dress.

"Hmmm." She might have to sell that, but if anyone could do it, she could.

The smile was still on her lips when she moved the magazine aside and saw the first piece of mail. The envelope was plain. White. With no return address.

Lila shook her head. It looked like an envelope that had contained some of those letters that protested her policies and decisions. But that couldn't be. Tim had sent those, just as he'd done those things to Bailey.

Maybe it was something from Zach.

Just the day before he'd sent her a thank-you note because she'd gotten him some autographed cards from the Dallas Mavericks basketball team. Yes, it was probably another thank-you card.

It was silly to think the worst.

She ran the letter opener across the top of the envelope and pulled out the note card tucked inside. Lila read the four words of the handwritten message, and she gasped, dropping the note back on her desk. She moved away from it as quickly as she could.

"Oh, God." And Lila kept repeating it as she reached for the phone to call Bart.

She couldn't take her eyes off the note, and the words stared back at her, taunting her.

"Lila," Bart answered.

She didn't bother with a greeting. "I got another note," she told him, hating the fear in her voice and hating even more that the fear had her by the throat.

It wasn't over.

It wasn't over at all.

"I'll send someone to pick it up," Bart assured her.

"It's the worst one yct," Lila managed to say. And because she didn't know what else to do, she read the words aloud.

"Time to die, Lila."

* * * * *

COMING NEXT MONTH

Available May 10, 2011

#1275 BABY BOOTCAMP
Daddy Corps
Mallory Kane

#1276 BRANDED
Whitehorse, Montana: Chisholm Cattle Company
B.J. Daniels

#1277 DAMAGED
Colby Agency: The New Equalizers
Debra Webb

#1278 THE MAN FROM GOSSAMER RIDGE
Cooper Justice: Cold Case Investigation
Paula Graves

#1279 UNFORGETTABLE
Cassie Miles

#1280 BEAR CLAW CONSPIRACY
Bear Claw Creek Crime Lab
Jessica Andersen

With an evil force hell-bent on destruction, two enemies must unite to find a truth that turns all-too-personal when passions collide.

Enjoy a sneak peek in Jenna Kernan's next installment in her original TRACKER *series, GHOST STALKER, available in May, only from Harlequin Nocturne.*

"Who are you?" he snarled.

Jessie lifted her chin. "Your better."

His smile was cold. "Such arrogance could only come from a Niyanoka."

She nodded. "Why are you here?"

"I don't know." He glanced about her room. "I asked the birds to take me to a healer."

"And they have done so. Is that *all* you asked?"

"No. To lead them away from my friends." His eyes fluttered and she saw them roll over white.

Jessie straightened, preparing to flee, but he roused himself and mastered the momentary weakness. His eyes snapped open, locking on her.

Her heart hammered as she inched back.

"Lead who away?" she whispered, suddenly afraid of the answer.

"The ghosts. Nagi sent them to attack me so I would bring them to her."

The wolf must be deranged because Nagi did not send ghosts to attack living creatures. He captured the evil ones after their death if they refused to walk the Way of Souls, forcing them to face judgment.

"Her? The healer you seek is also female?"

"Michaela. She's Niyanoka, like you. The last Seer of Souls and Nagi wants her dead."

Jessie fell back to her seat on the carpet as the possibility of this ricocheted in her brain. Could it be true?

"Why should I believe you?" But she knew why. His black aura, the part that said he had been touched by death. Only a ghost could do that. But it made no sense.

Why would Nagi hunt one of her people and why would a Skinwalker want to protect her? She had been trained from birth to hate the Skinwalkers, to consider them a threat.

His intent blue eyes pinned her. Jessie felt her mouth go dry as she considered the impossible. Could the trickster be speaking the truth? Great Mystery, what evil was this?

She stared in astonishment. There was only one way to find her answers. But she had never even met a Skinwalker before and so did not even know if they dreamed.

But if he dreamed, she would have her chance to learn the truth.

Look for GHOST STALKER by Jenna Kernan, available May only from Harlequin Nocturne, wherever books and ebooks are sold.

HNEXP0511

Harlequin
INTRIGUE
WILL THE QUEST FOR THE KILLERS BE TOO MUCH FOR THIS TOWN TO HANDLE?
FIND OUT IN THE NEWEST MINISERIES BY USA TODAY BESTSELLING AUTHOR
B.J. DANIELS
WHITEHORSE MONTANA
Chisholm Cattle Company
Colton Chisholm has lived with the guilt of not helping his high-school sweetheart when she needed him most. Fourteen years later, he's committed to finding out what happened to her the night she disappeared. The same night he stood her up.
BRANDED
May 2011
Five more titles to follow....
www.eHarlequin.com

HI69543